SAVING SYCAMORE BAY

CAMI CHECKETTS

BIRCH CREEK PUBLISHING

COPYRIGHT

Saving Her Plantation: Destined for Love: Mansions

Copyright © 2017 by Cami Checketts

DEDICATION

To my football-loving husband! It's so fun to write a novel where I can bug you with really important questions like, Would a cornerback or an outside linebacker have better-looking biceps?

FREE BOOK

Sign up for Cami's newsletter and find out about new releases and sales. Also receive a free ebook copy of *The Resilient One: A Billionaire Bride Pact Romance* here.

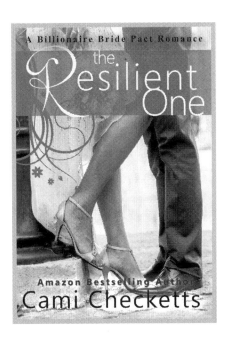

1

Harrison Jackson smoothed his brand spanking new navy-blue suit coat, checked his tie, and rapped on the boss's door. Was the rap too hard and demanding, too soft and wimpy? *Come on, man, calm down.* Yet it was hard to calm down. First day on the job with Goodman and Giles Accounting Firm in downtown Montgomery and he was being called into the owner's office. He had no inkling if it was a good thing or a bad thing, but his stomach was in knots and his palms were sweating. He felt like he was waiting to run out onto the field before a home football game. Those last few seconds before running down the tunnel were almost worse than warm-ups. He just wanted to be in the game, not waiting for it.

"Come in," Mr. Goodman called.

Harrison eased the door open and stepped inside. *Keep those shoulders back*, he remembered. It was his mama's voice, and he really needed it right now. He straightened his back and gave a forced smile. "You wanted to see me, sir?"

Mr. Goodman's face split into a smile with teeth almost as

bright as his bald head. He stood and offered his hand, pumping Harrison's larger hand with his. He was within an inch of Harrison's six-four, but half as thick. "Come in, son, have a seat." He gestured toward the leather chair. The office had a great view of the Riverwalk and downtown Montgomery; the water was peaceful today and the sun shone off the glassy surface.

Harrison resisted rubbing his sweaty palms on his clean pants and wished he could be peaceful like the water, but not shining. He hated it when his forehead and nose got shiny—a neon sign announcing his nervousness. Why had he imagined in college that he could roll with the heavy hitters in the world of accounting? He loved numbers and people, but sometimes his confidence faltered around the ultra-wealthy and powerful. You'd think he'd be used to those types by now, since they'd financed his schooling and wanted to chat with him after every Auburn football game, to be his buddy because he could knock another player on his butt.

"We're so thrilled that you've joined Goodman and Giles, Harrison."

"Thank you, sir."

"Call me Henry, please."

"Um, yes, sir, Henry." Harrison's tongue was all twisted and his eyes were wide. Why was the boss asking him to call him by his first name?

"I have a question for you, son."

"Shoot. I mean, sure. Ask away." He rubbed his palms on his pants before he could stop himself.

Mr. Goodman—er, Henry—took a long breath. "Do you like adventure, Harrison?"

"Adventure? Sure, who doesn't like adventure?" He chuckled nervously. He'd chosen to get a master's in accounting. Didn't that basically scream you had no desire for adventure? His sister Moriah, she was all over adventure, and she and her new husband, Jace, were traveling the globe taking in all the adventure their son Turk could handle. Harrison was happier at home—working hard at school and playing football with his buddies on any break he had. Sure, he hated sitting hour after hour, but someday he'd be able to afford a stand-up desk. Then his life would be close to perfect.

"I have a crazy proposition for you, son."

Harrison's back was now dripping sweat to match his palms. He just wanted to crunch numbers and be polite to clients, maybe coach a youth football team in his free time. Was that too much to ask?

"My best friend passed away last month."

"My condolences, sir."

Henry nodded. "His daughter is all alone in this world and I promised I'd take care of her." He paused as if Harrison should say something.

"That's very honorable of you."

"It would be if I could actually do it." He picked up a pen and clicked it a few times, glaring out the window at the picturesque view. "I've got to do right by her and she needs someone ... someone strong, young, and able to stand up for her." He focused back on Harrison and nodded like Harrison was a prized stud horse that was going to make him a fortune.

Harrison had seen that look in many a coach's eye. He didn't like it. Sometimes it made him feel like the supermodel who kept trying to tell the world she had a brain, but nobody could see past her face.

"I've prayed long and hard about this, and you're my answer, son," Henry said.

"Answer to what?" Harrison tugged at his tie. This conversation was causing him more stress than studying for the CPA had. At least his boss was a praying man. That gave him some comfort.

"I can't leave Montgomery. My wife's kidneys are failing and she has to have dialysis three times a week." He shook his head sadly. "My kids are all out in the world—doing great, mind you, but not any help to me with their mama or with our sweet Grace. Bless that girl's heart. All alone in the world ... and something nefarious is going on, I tell you. She's thinking about selling the family home to a shyster, and there is no reason for it. The money should be there. Her daddy wouldn't have left her without enough money to survive and care for their estate. I've checked all the books and the money's there in the estate, but there is something wrong with the will. It's my belief they're trying to force her to sell or marry that loser Beau. Oh, I tell you! I don't trust the lawyers involved any more than a snake in the grass. Do you understand what I'm saying, son?"

Harrison stared at him and tried to recap the surprising emotional outburst. He'd always thought his boss was calm and collected. "Your friend's daughter is in trouble and you can't help?"

"Yes! You've got it. So you'll go help her?" Henry leaned forward eagerly. "I'll pay you double your salary, and when you come back to Montgomery I'll give you a dream list of clients—*my* clients. I need to start stepping down anyway and take better care of Maribelle. I promise I will make this worth your while, son. Thank you so much for being willing to help."

Harrison had no clue when he'd agreed to help. Double his salary sounded nice—okay, better than nice—and taking over Henry's clients would be a dream. But how could he just pack up and go ... where exactly and for how long? "Wh-where is Grace, and what can I do to help?"

Henry sprung up from his chair, rushed around, and pulled Harrison to his feet, shaking his hand again and slapping him on the back. "Oh, thank you, son, thank you!" He paused to wipe at his eyes.

Harrison looked away, giving the man a moment to compose himself and wondering what he'd gotten himself into. He was trying to ask questions, not commit, but here he was like a sheep stuck in quicksand.

"The family home is just outside of Mobile, down near the water. Beautiful spot," Mr. Goodman continued. "You're such an answer to prayers. I told Maribelle that you were *it*. That you could protect Grace from whatever is happening in that house, and that you were smart enough to fix her financial problems too. Bless you, son, bless you."

Harrison couldn't even think of a response.

2

Grace Addison looked around Sycamore Bay, her family's ancestral mansion, morosely. She'd worked since five a.m. and still hadn't made much progress painting the trim in the formal dining room—if only there wasn't so blasted much area to paint. The white trim was everywhere, a great contrast to the blue-gray walls, but oh my, it was exhausting. Every day of the past month had been the same: she rose early and scrubbed, painted, tried to restore, fix, or maintain something on the house and keep up the yard as well, but she was falling further and further behind. Finishing up her master's in school counseling seemed like a faraway dream.

Beau made fun of her for trying so hard, but she loved this house almost as much as she'd loved her daddy. She smiled and crossed herself. Rest his wonderful soul.

But that stinking Beau ... if they hadn't been friends since they were born, she'd tell him to go crawl in a hole. Their mamas had been best friends, but now they were both gone—his mama to a horrific car accident and her mama to cancer. Now her daddy was gone too. She and Beau were basically alone in the world, because his daddy didn't deserve the term of endearment. She had her high school friends, college friends, and friends from church who all cared, but Beau had always been there. Well, most of the time it'd been the other way around, and she'd taken care of him after his daddy whooped his rear, but now Beau was back home from college, too, and had promised he'd help her save her beloved house.

The doorbell rang, and she clenched the paintbrush tighter. It was either somebody telling her she owed them money or Beau here to tease her about working like a commoner. She'd show him common, paint a stripe right down his perfect nose.

Setting the paintbrush on the tray, she tried to straighten her shirt and her hair, but what could she possibly do with the blonde curls tied up in a kerchief and paint splattered all over an old Auburn U football T-shirt? She sighed. Her days of screaming for her favorite football players seemed long, long ago.

She hurried across the grand entry and swung the door wide. "H-hello," she said, the annoyance in her voice fizzling out to a reverent whisper.

Standing on her threshold was the most handsome man she'd ever seen in real life. He was no stranger to her, as she'd cheered for him every weekend in the fall. His deep brown skin was smooth and his lips were just awe-inspiring—full, shapely, and so delectable. She and her roommate, Isabelle, used to stay up late at nights discussing what it would be like to kiss those lips. Then there were his deep brown eyes, the type that made a woman want to stare into them for hours. Not to mention his tall, well-built frame. Ooh, she could just picture him in his football uniform. Here he stood on her front porch, dressed in a deep blue suit and smiling apprehensively at her. If possible, he'd gotten even more handsome since last fall. What was he doing on her doorstep? Lord have mercy.

"Good morning, ma'am," he said all formal-like, sticking out his hand. "I'm Harrison Jackson."

"I know who you are," she breathed out. She put her hand in his and felt for a moment like she'd found heaven. "Number twenty-two, best cornerback in the NCAA."

Harrison let out a grunt that sounded like a laugh and retrieved his hand. "Um, thank you, ma'am."

Her eyes widened and she wagged a finger at him. "Don't you act like it isn't true. I watched every game of your college career and I know you're the top, just like my mama's pecan pie is the best in the South." Well, used to be the best in the South.

This time he did laugh, a deep chuckle that warmed her clear through to her toes. "I appreciate the compliment, ma'am, but if I'd been the best I would've been drafted, not working as an accountant." He grinned, and those white teeth flashing against his dark skin made her feel a bit faint. "Not that I'm complaining. Accounting's a good career, lots of opportunity."

She eyed him up and down. That fit body was going to be stuck behind a desk all day? That was like cooping up a snow leopard or a tiger. "No, no, no. You can't be an accountant. You are a football player, you must play!"

Harrison laughed again. "I'm fine, really, ma'am. I'm doing what I want to do."

She eyed him, confused by his response and not sure he was being square with her, but then a bigger question begged an answer. "What are you doing on my front porch?"

His smile dimmed. "Mr. Goodman sent me."

Henry. Her dad's best friend. He was like an uncle to her. He and her Uncle Mike, her daddy's former right-hand man, were better uncles than any of her blood relatives. "Is Maribelle doing all right?"

"Not really, ma'am. Mr. Goodman felt his place was with her during her dialysis. But he has a lot of ..." His mouth twisted as he searched for the right word. "*Concern* for you, so he sent me to help."

Henry had just become her favorite person. He cared enough to send help and to send it with style. Harrison Jackson. It was like a superstar walking right through her front door. How long was he planning to help? If she could talk him into staying in one of the eight bedrooms upstairs, maybe she'd get some rest at night. Nobody and nothing was going to get through all of those muscles.

Grace stepped back, blushing at the thought of him sleeping in the next room over. "Where are my manners? Come in, let me get you a glass of lemonade."

"Thank you, ma'am."

They walked side by side back to the kitchen. Her mama would be appalled that she didn't care about having a guest sit in the formal room and bring him refreshment, but Grace was tired —tired of the pomp and circumstance, tired of serving and work- ing, and just all around tired. She'd worked her tail end off. If she wanted to sit in her sunny kitchen and drink lemonade next to this fine-looking man, she'd ignore her mama's censure from heaven.

She glanced up, way up, to Harrison's strong jawline. He must've felt her gaze, because he gazed down at her. His slow grin made her stomach tumble. "You are Grace Addison, correct? I kind of assumed."

Grace laughed and gestured to her paint-covered clothing. "You probably thought you'd find me dressed a little classier than this."

They made it to the kitchen and Harrison held the swinging

door open for her. Just the sight of his strong body and that arm holding the door made her feel faint again. Maybe having him stay here wasn't such a good idea. She'd never get anything accomplished besides ogling him.

"Truth be told, ma'am, I kind of envisioned a big old hoop skirt with your hair in curls and you daintily holding a teacup."

Grace loved the teasing lilt to his voice. "Gracious me, sir, I'll go put on my corset and hoops right now." She laid the Southern drawl on thick enough to frost a cake.

Harrison's deep chuckle reverberated through the large kitchen, filling up all the nooks and crannies that had survived without laughter this past month. She smiled in return, falling completely in love with his laugh, and gestured to a chair by the butcher-block table. As a child, she'd spent many an hour in here with their cook and close family friend, Aunt Geraldine, and her mama. Generations before, the prejudice was thick, but her parents had dispelled with all of that. They loved their employees like family, which worked well since they all lived and worked under the same roof. Grace had been raised by Aunt Geraldine as surely as her mama, but with money as tight as it was now, she'd had to let everyone go when her daddy died. Aunt Geraldine and her husband, Uncle Mike, claimed they were ready to retire anyway. Luckily Daddy had set up a fund for them that the lawyers couldn't touch and they'd bought a little house a few miles down the beach.

Grace tried to understand why her daddy hadn't done the same for her. Her lawyer, Ike, was a very nice man who patiently explained things to her, but he couldn't change the twenty-year-old will any more than she could. She was only allowed two thousand dollars a month to live and maintain Sycamore Bay, unless she either sold the house, married, or turned thirty. Thirty was a few years off, marriage probably further than that, and she'd work two jobs before she sold her house. Two thousand dollars a month would've been a fortune twenty years ago, or even back in her college days, but she was finding it wasn't much to maintain a house and property. She was still making payments to the plumber for the septic tank backing up into the main floor bathroom, and it would take a year to get on top of the bill the electrician had left in her mailbox for updating the outlets to the fridge and stove after they shorted out two months ago. Uncle Mike used to maintain the place, but when she went away to college, Uncle Mike must've gotten overwhelmed and worn out. Things were pretty run-down.

Harrison sat and she went to the fridge, coming back with a tall pitcher of lemonade and pouring two glasses full. Sadly, she had no cookies, pie, or anything sweet to serve with it. Her mama was definitely rolling over in her grave right about now.

"Thank you." Harrison took the glass in his large palm and drained a long swallow. "Warm today."

"You should take that suit coat off." Grace reddened, partially because of her implication that she'd like him to take clothes off, but also because she couldn't afford the air conditioning, so she'd turned it off. It was a warm June day in the South, well over eighty with way too much humidity and no breeze to hope on. "I mean, if you want to."

Harrison simply smiled at her and shrugged out of his suit coat, placing it on the back of his chair. Grace watched in awe, her jaw gaping slightly. His white shirt was short-sleeved, so his beautiful biceps were on fine display.

"I remember every time you intercepted the ball," she said dreamily, luckily catching herself before she told him everything she remembered: those large hands snatching the ball out of the air, his biceps bulging through his football uniform ...

"You really were a fan."

"Oh yes, sir. Never missed a home game, and watched all the away games on the TV." When he shifted as if her admission embarrassed him, she asked, "Do you miss it?"

"Oh yeah. I loved playing." He shrugged and took another drink, gripping the glass tightly. "But we all have to grow up at some point."

Her enthusiasm deflated. Harrison should still be playing football and she should still be enjoying college life, but here they were. He was a professional businessman and she was a professional painter and maintenance woman. Ha.

"What did you graduate in?" he asked, smiling at her.

Dang, he seemed like a nice guy. Who would've thought it? She'd dated a few athletes in college and some of them had heads bigger than their stats. Harrison should've been like that, but he definitely wasn't.

"I have a bachelor's of education and I was halfway through my master's when Daddy passed." She gestured around sadly. "It was either come home and take care of things, or lose Sycamore Bay to some jokers who want to tear it down and build a massive resort." She gestured out the large windows at the sweeping back lawn, which overlooked a gorgeous beach on Mobile Bay. Oak trees lined the property, almost a hundred acres of grass, forest, and swampland. She couldn't even keep the grass around the house mowed and trimmed. The flower beds were a mess and the rest of the property was overgrown. Hopefully her poor mama couldn't really look down on her from heaven, though Grace always felt like she was.

"I'm sorry about your daddy." He guzzled the rest of his lemonade and casually reclined into the chair.

"It is what it is." She fought back the tears, brushing at one that she didn't catch fast enough. "So what did Henry send you to do?"

He glanced away and rubbed at his neck. She'd most likely

embarrassed him with her emotion. "Well, he wanted me to help with your financial trouble and whatever else you need."

She cocked her head to the side. "How long does he expect you to stay?"

"Until the job's done." His gaze met hers again.

"Like, stay here in the house? With me?" She swallowed and lowered her voice. "Please." *Please say yes, please say yes*. Did she sound too needy, or not needy enough? She didn't want to make him uncomfortable, but if Henry had sent him, she knew she could trust him. She'd really, truly love to have someone around for protection, help, company. Being alone was miserable, and sometimes downright terrifying. Sometimes she heard strange noises in the night or saw lights down on her beach. Her daddy's gun was a small reassurance, but luckily no one had tried to come into the house yet.

"If that's all right with you, ma'am. I don't want to make you uncomfortable."

"The ma'am-ing is making me uncomfortable." She smiled. "But I'd be much obliged to have you here. I'm struggling." That was about as much as she could admit to at this moment. She was so far past struggling. She was drowning in loneliness, sorrow, and despair, and had no clue how to balance preserving her heritage and finding a life for herself someday.

He nodded solemnly, and they stood. "Well, then, put me to work, ma'am—I mean, Grace." He said her name a bit uncomfortably.

"What kind of work were you expecting to do?"

"I can do anything you need—maintenance, yard work, my mama taught me how to cook. I'm not great at painting, but I can learn." He gestured to her paint-splattered self and smiled. Oh, his teeth were well taken care of. She wanted to write his dentist a thank-you note.

"In that suit?" Grace looked over his six-foot-four glory. She would never want to get him dirty in that fabulous suit.

"I clean up right nice."

"Yes, you do." And that was much too forward.

"I meant, I can get dirty and I'll clean up—not that I think I look good in the suit." He blew out a breath. "That came out all wrong."

She couldn't help but laugh. "You are not at all what I expected."

"How so?" He cocked his head to the side.

"Watching you play. You never seemed cocky like some of the other guys, but I just assumed you would be because of how amazing you play and how good-looking you ..." She bit at her lip, wishing she could bite off her tongue. "Whew. Time to stop talking."

Harrison gave her a slow grin. "It's all right. I'll take compliments from a pretty lady any day."

That got her laughing again. As scrubby as she looked right now, she knew he was just teasing her. "Do you have your things outside?" she asked.

"Yes, ma'am."

She swatted at him. "Call me ma'am again and I'll make you sleep in the attic." She blushed, knowing she couldn't really threaten him with anything. He was here helping her, and she was in deep debt to him already.

"I can sleep anywhere, ma'am." He dropped his voice low and his deep brown eyes twinkled at her. Those eyes could be soulful, mirthful, sexiful. Wait, that wasn't a word.

She glanced over him. "Big guy like you needs a good bed." She could not believe they were teasing about beds, of all things. A tingle shot up her spine. Harrison Jackson was going to be sleeping in her house. Oh goodness. She needed to call Isabelle and squeal about this or something.

He shrugged. "I'm easy to please."

Grace thought she'd better curtail the flirting before she revealed exactly how infatuated she was with him. She hurried in front of him and pushed the kitchen door open. He was quick, darting to the door and holding it for her. Of course he was quick; he was Harrison Jackson. She gave him a faltering smile and strode down the hallway.

Henry Goodman had promised her daddy he'd take care of her, but he'd sent Harrison as his replacement. Henry deserved a lot of blessings right now. She'd quadruple her prayers for him and Maribelle.

3

Harrison kept sneaking glances at Grace as they painted white trim throughout the main living areas. He'd had no inkling what to expect coming here, but she had exceeded every scenario he'd run through his mind during the two-and-a-half-hour drive. It wasn't just that she was beautiful and a fan of his football career, though both of those were nice bonuses. It was the sparkle in her blue eyes as she teased with him; the resilience in the set of her smooth jaw, even though she'd been through so many hard things; the way she had her blonde curls tied back in a sloppy ponytail like she wasn't trying to impress anyone. He loved that she was painting and trying to maintain this enormous house and property. She was a lot tougher than he thought she'd be, and he'd really like to hold her close and reassure her that he would help her through this ... but he was getting way ahead of himself even thinking that. Still, what an hour ago had been an uncertain and unwelcome step toward job promotion was already becoming a personal quest to help Grace.

A hard rap came at the door, and a man shouted through it. "Gracie Lee, your favorite *stud* in the world is here!"

Grace rolled her eyes and set her paintbrush on the tray. "Pardon me, please."

Harrison nodded, trying not to look crestfallen. A boyfriend? Why hadn't he realized that Grace would have someone? He'd only known her an hour and he'd already considered campaigning for the job of boyfriend if it was open. Apparently it wasn't. The disappointment shouldn't slice so painfully. He barely knew her. He kept painting the whiteboard as carefully as he could, but still he hit the main part of the wall much too often. Grace had told him that they'd paint that part next, so it was no worry. Hopefully his painting skills would improve by then. The brush felt too small for his big palms.

As Grace and the maybe-boyfriend spoke, their voices carried easily to the formal dining room, where he didn't even try to not listen in.

"What on the Lord's green earth are you doing?" the man asked before Grace even said hello. "You act like you're a slave or something."

Harrison's hackles rose. If this was Grace's boyfriend, she definitely needed an upgrade.

"Back off, Beau, or I'll paint a stripe down your face so everyone knows what a skunk you are."

This Beau guy laughed. "There's my little spicy girl. Seriously, darlin', why do you work yourself to the bone when you know I'll take care of you? Sell this dump and move in with me—or better yet, marry me. We'll have bundles of money and no worries but how you're going to make me happy."

Harrison set his paintbrush down and stood. Who was this joker, and what right did he have to tell Grace what to do?

"Don't you ever call my house a dump. You claim you want to

help me, but marrying you is definitely *not* the help I need. All you do is poke fun at me. Get your sorry carcass out of here!"

Harrison figured it was time. He strode toward the front entry before his good sense could talk him out of it.

"Aw, come on, baby. Don't be like that. You know I just love you ..." The guy's voice trailed off as he spotted Harrison. He was a slicked-back preppy guy with the collar of his golf shirt turned up and tanned legs and arms showing. Country clubs and daddy's money were all too evident. Harrison disliked him at first glance.

"What the ..." Fortunately Beau muttered the expletive under his breath. "How did *he* get here?"

Grace turned and drew in a shaky breath, leaning against the doorjamb as her eyes met Harrison's. "This is Harrison Jackson. All-star cornerback for the Auburn Tigers." She beamed proudly at him, and his chest swelled from her obvious adoration.

Beau arched an eyebrow and brushed his hand through his blond hair. His icy blue eyes swept over Harrison. "I know *who* he is, Gracie. The thing I don't know is why he's playing maintenance man at your house."

Harrison bit back a retort and stepped forward with his hand extended. "Nice to meet you."

Beau stared at his hand for half a beat before slowly lifting his arm and giving him a quick, limp handshake, as if Harrison would soil him with paint or something more sinister. "You had a great season last fall," Beau spit out. "Too bad nobody from the NFL thought so."

Harrison's jaw tightened and he had to force a smile. "It was fun while it lasted. Did you go to Auburn?"

Beau nodded shortly. "Graduated with this princess, but she thinks she's Cinderella or something."

Grace stuck her tongue out at him, then turned to Harrison. "You'll have to forgive his atrocious manners. Beau's been my friend since we were in the womb, and he thinks he can act like a brother and tell me what to do."

Beau stared at her. "You've never thought of me as a brother, and we're way past friends, little girl."

Grace blushed. "In your dreams."

"Every night," he countered.

Harrison was feeling decidedly uncomfortable, and he suddenly realized that he hated this Beau guy. It was too strong for barely meeting the dude, and Harrison usually got along well with everyone. Even in grade school, when there'd been some strong racial prejudice, he'd found ways to tease about it and make friends, but Beau just rubbed him wrong. Maybe it was because the guy had pointed, out in front of Grace, Harrison's failure to play football at the next level, but it was more likely that Harrison was worried that Beau and Grace really were "way past friends."

"Harrison and I need to get back to work. If you'll excuse us ..." Grace turned to walk away.

Beau grabbed her wrist and yanked her toward him. She cried out.

Harrison used his speed and strength to his advantage, and before Grace or Beau could react, he'd seized Beau's wrist and squeezed hard. The man released Grace and Harrison quickly put his body in front of her as a shield. It was pure caveman reaction, but he didn't care at the moment. He didn't say anything, but simply stared down at Beau.

"What is this?" Beau asked. "Grace is my girl, and I don't care who you think you are—you don't come in here and pull her away from me."

"I am *not* your girl." Grace moved around Harrison to glare at Beau. Harrison barely resisted wrapping his arm around her. It wasn't his place or his time, but he really, really wanted to protect her from this idiot.

Beau looked Harrison up and down, then turned the force of his glare on Grace. "So that's how you're going to play it? I've been here for you your entire life, but some big-name, overly muscled football player comes along and you just push me away?"

Grace lifted her chin. "You picked this fight, Beau. I'm not selling my house to your daddy, and I'm *not* moving in with you or marrying you. When you're ready to be my friend again, a real friend who is there for me and isn't pushing me into things I'm not comfortable with, you know where I am." She stepped back. Harrison released Beau's wrist and backed up next to her right as Grace slammed the door in Beau's face.

He turned to her with a smile of congratulations on being so strong, but her beautiful blue eyes were swimming in tears and her lip was trembling. "Oh, hey, hey." Harrison couldn't resist any longer. He wrapped his arms around her back and pulled her against his chest. She sort of moaned in relief, and Harrison found his arms holding her closer. Her body was strong yet soft—the perfect mix of femininity and athleticism, in his opinion. He'd been pretty busy with football and fitting five years of schooling into four with getting his master's degree during the time he had a football scholarship, so he hadn't dated a lot, but plenty of girls had come on to him. Grace in his arms felt more right than any woman ever had.

Grace burrowed her head into his chest and hugged him back. Harrison cradled her there. He wasn't really the type of guy to mutter sweet nothings, but he felt like this was the time to say something. "Hey, it's okay. I'm here, I'm here." He repeated a few times.

Grace sighed softly, but didn't respond besides clinging to him tighter. Harrison gently rubbed his hands up and down her back. She smelled like an interesting combination of paint fumes and sweet vanilla. Several blissful minutes of holding her passed before she sniffled and raised her head, pulling back slightly. "I'm sorry. You probably think I'm the biggest wimp ever."

"I think you're tougher than anyone I know. Except maybe my mama, but she's kind of scary tough."

She laughed softly and wiped under her eyes. Shaking her head, she pulled away, and Harrison felt like he had to let her go. They stood there in the entryway. Grace wouldn't meet his gaze, and he didn't know her well enough to force her to talk to him or force her back into his arms like he really wanted.

Finally, he couldn't resist asking because he was afraid she was crying because she really did love the guy. "So you and Beau ..." *Please say no, please say no.*

"Are not together and never have been." She blew out a breath. "He thinks he owns me sometimes, but he really is a good person." She lowered her voice and muttered, "Sometimes. It's one of those difficult, family friend type of deals, and Beau's been through a lot. You know how that goes?"

Harrison smiled, thinking of how his mama would react if any kind of friend treated someone the way Beau had just treated Grace. She'd be reaming Harrison out right now for not knocking the kid on his butt.

She pulled her fingers through her long curls and then twisted a lock around her index finger. Harrison's mouth went dry, and he wondered how that hair would feel with his hands tangled in it. *Focus.* "So you put up with him because of your family, or his?"

"Our mamas were best friends. They grew up together and so Beau and I grew up together. Our daddies tolerated each other. They did some business deals, but my daddy didn't really like working with Mr. Steele."

Harrison rubbed a hand over his head, getting a bad feeling in his gut. "Mr. Goodman wanted me to look over all your financials and figure out why your money's tied up. Does any of that have to do with Mr. Steele?"

Grace's eyes widened. "It shouldn't, but I could show you everything I have. Do you want to do that now?"

"You know how I love numbers." He winked.

Grace smiled, and it reassured him that she was okay now. "Giving up football to crunch numbers. Crazy."

He laughed, but wondered if he needed to set her straight, if Beau's snide comment hadn't already showcased how he'd failed. He would've kept playing football if anybody in the NFL would've offered him a decent contract. He wasn't quite big enough physically to play his position at the next level, and he knew that, but it was still tough to swallow. Several of his friends were still trying to live the dream, working out every spare minute and going to every Pro Day and hoping an NFL scout would notice them and pick them up. Harrison would've enjoyed playing more, but that wasn't the Lord's plan for him and he was okay with that, most of the time.

"Why don't we finish painting the trim, and then I can look over whatever paperwork you have here and make some calls if I need?" he asked.

"Sounds good. I'll clean myself up and fry you some catfish and grits."

His stomach rumbled. He'd eaten this morning but skipped lunch. "You are a true Southern girl."

She winked and saucily flipped her hair. "And don't you forget it."

4

Since Grace's daddy died, she'd been certain that her life was cursed, but apparently Mama had pushed her weight around in heaven long enough and sent an angel to her. She settled into her bed and smiled, not sure if angels were supposed to be as fine-looking as Harrison or make a girl's heart thump quite as much, but they were probably all as kind and thoughtful as him. Ahh. The fact that he was only a few bedrooms over was going to make it difficult to sleep tonight. When he'd cradled her in his arms after Beau's rudeness, she'd had that wonderful feeling that she wasn't alone anymore and it still warmed her.

They'd spent the evening looking through the will, the papers from the lawyers, and all of the bank statements. It should have been miserable, but it wasn't because he was there. He smelled like man. Not necessarily some particular cologne, but clean and outdoorsy and just yummy. When he brushed against her arm a few times, she'd had to force her breathing back to normal.

Sadly, Harrison had to agree that the will didn't look to have any wiggle room. She was only allowed the two thousand dollars a month until she got married or turned thirty, and then she'd have complete control of all the funds—funds totaling over twenty million dollars. The property itself was worth an extra five. The investment company that was after it had offered her five point two million, but she had no desire to sell. This was the place she wanted to welcome lost children who needed a place to live and belong, who needed her.

Yet how in the world was she going to keep paying the bills, maintaining this place, and scraping enough food together for two thousand dollars a month? She would never get the Alabama Department of Human Resources to award her any foster children living by herself with no money and a house that was falling down around her head.

She was baffled that her daddy would do this to her. She'd argued with the lawyer, Ike, that he'd meant to put another zero on the end of that monthly stipend. The lawyer had kindly explained that her daddy hadn't wanted her to have a lump sum of money until she was old enough to make smart choices. He told her that her daddy had most likely meant for her to find a husband because he didn't want her to be alone, and then he not so smartly suggested that Beau Steele would be perfect for the job. Grace may have given a completely unladylike snort and sneer that shocked her lawyer, as he had known her mama. Beau and her? Not happening.

The real truth of the matter was, her daddy hadn't thought he was going to die and hadn't updated his will in over twenty years, since she was a baby. Back then, two thousand dollars a month was a lot of money and the property had been in much better shape. He also probably thought he'd live well past her thirtieth birthday and give her hand away in marriage. She sighed, but luckily her eyes stayed dry. She'd cried enough about her loss.

Grace heard a cough from outside her open second-story

window and then saw a flash of light. She scrambled out of her covers and to her window. The light moved off toward the beach. Who was on her property? She'd been alone the past month and a half, and although she didn't like it, she'd grown pretty brave. Pulling her daddy's 1911 out of the drawer, she loaded in several bullets, then hurried from her room, holding the gun to her side. She slipped quietly down the back staircase and into some shoes next to the kitchen door.

Suddenly she stopped. She'd completely forgotten there was a buff, intimidating-looking man sleeping upstairs. Should she yell for him? She pushed open the door and scanned the yard. She'd yell if she got in trouble. Her daddy had taught her how to take care of herself.

She headed toward the beach, but couldn't see the light anymore. There was a slip of a moon, but not enough to know if someone was lying in wait for her behind the knotty trunk of a cypress tree or out in the wetlands. She hated feeling so vulnerable and suddenly she felt exposed in a tank top and cut-off sweats, even with the reassurance of the weapon cradled in her palm.

"Grace," a deep voice whispered too close.

Grace whirled and pulled the gun up, aiming for the man's chest.

"Whoa! It's me." Harrison stepped back and put his hands up. The faint light of the moon kissed his smooth, brown skin, but his dark eyes were hard to read right now.

Grace lowered the gun, her hand shaking from the adrenaline rush and the terror of realizing she could've shot him. "Oh, Harrison. I'm sorry."

"My fault. Remind me not to sneak up on you."

"You are scary sneaky."

"Perfected the art of scaring my sister." He winked, but stepped close and lowered his voice. "Did you see somebody?"

"Yes. Did you?" She instinctively leaned toward him, and the trembling seemed to calm.

He nodded. "I followed the light down to the beach, but they took off in a boat."

"Oh. That makes sense." She blew out a breath, and her fingers relaxed on the trigger and she clicked the thumb safety back into place. At least whoever had been here was gone, but why was somebody here? Just teenagers messing around, or was it something more sinister?

"Let's get you inside," Harrison said, his voice calm and even, the steady reassurance she needed right now. He wrapped his arm around her, and his bare chest brushed her shoulder. Why didn't he have a shirt on? Heaven help her. All thoughts of a trespasser fled as she could feel his muscles pressed against her.

"Do you always sleep half-naked?" she couldn't help but ask as they walked through the kitchen door and she flipped a light on, turning to face him.

Harrison coughed out a laugh. "Um ... yeah. Does it bother you? I can sleep in a shirt."

"It doesn't bother me." She shook her head quickly and couldn't help glancing at the fine display of muscles covered with smooth, brown skin. "Football was good to you," she said, then blushed.

Harrison chuckled.

"I'm going to make some chamomile tea," she blurted out. "Would you like some?"

"Sure." He locked the back door behind them and settled onto a barstool next to the wide butcher-block island.

Grace set the gun on the counter and hurried to fill a kettle with water, feeling awkward that Harrison was watching her every move with her hair pulled back in a ponytail and wearing beat-up clothes. Then again, that was how she'd looked when he'd met her and he hadn't seemed to care.

She set the kettle on the stove and pushed the button to ignite the burner.

"Did you do a sport in college?" he asked.

"No. Why do you ask?" Grace turned, pressing her hands behind her and leaning against the countertop.

"You're in great shape." He glanced away, and Grace liked him even more for the slight embarrassment after his compliment.

"Thanks. I love to run, placed in state in the two-hundred-yard dash, but I wasn't fast enough to run for Auburn." She turned around and busied herself putting tea bags in the cups, then filling them with the boiling water. Setting a cup in front of Harrison, she cradled her hands around her cup and sat on the stool next to him.

"Thank you," he said.

"Thank you for being here. I can't tell you how nice it is to not be alone." Her voice caught on the world *alone*. She was truly on her own in the world without her parents. Why couldn't they have had another child?

Harrison nudged her shoulder with his and bestowed that perfect smile on her. Ah, those teeth were white and straight, and even when he smiled his lips stayed full. "Happy to be here." His brow wrinkled. "I just wish I could be more help. Do you mind if we go visit the lawyer tomorrow and see what we can figure out?"

"Sure." But she doubted it would help at all.

He took a sip, then spoke quietly, almost like he was afraid she'd get upset. "I understand not wanting to sell because it's your family home, but it's a lot of house and property to maintain alone."

Alone. There was that word again. "I know, but I have some dreams and this is the perfect place for it."

He angled toward her, and her breath caught as she couldn't help but look over his muscled shoulders and chest, then allowed her eyes to dip down to his abdomen. Whoa, man, beautiful, beautiful man. "Care to share your dreams?"

She smiled at him and forced her gaze to meet his rather than focus so much on his physical attractiveness. He was a great guy, and that was much more important. "I want to do foster care. I want to fill Sycamore Bay with children who need a spot. I mean, look." She gestured around, even though it was dark outside. "There's so much room, and when Mama and Daddy were alive there was so much love. I always wanted brothers and sisters. So ... that's my dream."

Harrison simply stared at her, long enough that it got uncomfortable. He finally nodded and said, "I love your dream, Grace. I'll do all I can to help you."

Grace smiled, then took a sip of her tea. She didn't know him very well, but he loved her dream and would help her. She believed him. If anyone could help her, it would be Harrison Jackson.

5

Harrison was no stranger to hard work, but Grace seemed to thrive on it. They took a break from painting the next morning and started in on the overgrown yard. Harrison trimmed around the house and flower beds with a weed whacker, mowed the entire two acres of grass with a mower that wasn't self-propelled, and then cleared dead limbs throughout the edges of the forest and burned them. Grace tilled the vegetable garden and hand-weeded through more flower beds than he'd ever seen on a private property. She never slowed down and she never complained. She could've given the work ethic speech at football practice and maybe some of the lazier guys would've listened. He smirked. He knew he'd listen to anything she had to say.

They showered in the late afternoon and Harrison put his suit back on to go meet with the lawyer. When he exited his room, Grace was in the hallway. He stopped and just drank in the sight of her. A blousy red shirt and dark grey pencil skirt looked professional, yet feminine. Her shapely legs were showcased with heels that might give her the height to bring the top of her head to his chin. Her blue eyes seemed bigger with a little makeup on and her luscious lips were perfect in a shade of red like her shirt. Her long, blonde hair cascaded in curls down her back.

"Wow," Harrison managed. "If the lawyer tells you no, he needs his vision checked."

Grace flipped her hair over her shoulder and placed a hand on her hip. "Are you suggesting I'm going to get special privileges because of how I look?"

Yep, she and his sister, Moriah, would be the best of friends. Harrison smiled and took a step closer, feeling as bold as he did when the ball was in the air and the offense thought they were going to catch it, but he knew he was going to intercept and there was nothing they could do to stop him. "I'm saying you're the most beautiful, hard-working, and dedicated woman I've ever met, and I could never tell you no."

Grace's lips parted and then closed. Finally, she smiled. "I hope you don't have to ever tell me no, then."

Harrison chuckled and offered his arm. He escorted her to his new Hyundai Santa Fe Sport. He'd never had a car of his own, which was fine throughout high school as his parents had let him borrow their beat-up old Ford truck whenever he needed to drive. In college he'd been close enough to home, and busy enough with football and school, that it hadn't been an issue. But he was very proud to have his own vehicle now, and especially that it was new. His parents had never owned a new car. His dad had worked hard as an electrician and they'd always had enough but not a lot of extras. His parents and sister were insanely proud of him pushing his way through to his master's degree and getting a job with the most high-powered accounting firm in Montgomery.

He got Grace's door and she gave him a sweet smile before

sliding into the leather seat. Jogging around to the driver's side, he climbed in and pushed the start button.

"This is a nice car."

"Thank you." He smiled proudly and slid it into gear, driving down her tree-lined driveway.

"It seems too small for you, though."

"Too ... small?" She didn't like his car? His shoulders drooped.

She laughed. "Sorry. I didn't mean to insult you or anything. I just pictured you driving, like, a monster truck."

"Monster truck?" Harrison turned onto the main road leading toward downtown Mobile. "That doesn't feel very classy."

"You're right." She pursed her lips and angled toward him.

Harrison glanced over at her and his breath caught. He'd never seen anyone to rival her beauty, but it was the determination in her soul and the sweetness that radiated from her that made her irresistible.

"Yes, the monster truck definitely is not classy enough for you, but you need something big ..." Her eyes brightened and she snapped her fingers. "I've got it. A Hummer would fit you perfectly."

"A Hummer?" He scrunched up his forehead. He didn't have any problem with Hummers, but he really, really liked his Santa Fe. Did that make him wussy in her eyes? Nobody had ever suggested he was wussy.

"Or maybe a Range Rover or an Escalade."

Harrison could never afford a Range Rover or an Escalade. Well, maybe if he took over Mr. Goodman's clientele and was frugal for a few years. He shook his head. He didn't need to impress Grace with his car. If she cared that much about what he drove, she was shallow and not the woman for him.

He shook his head again. He barely knew her. What was he doing worrying if she was the woman for him?

Grace laughed. "You should see your face."

"What's my face doing?" Now she didn't like his vehicle or his face?

She reached up and smoothed the skin between his brow. His breath caught at the warmth of her fingers on his face. She trailed her fingers along the side of his face and across his jawline before pulling them back. "That handsome face is all scrunched up and worried. I'm just teasing you. I think your Santa Fe is great." She grinned. "You don't take teasing very well, do you?"

Harrison smiled, relieved. "My sister teased me every day of my life."

"Oh, good. I was worried you didn't know how to take a tease."

Harrison reached across the console and grabbed her hand. Her eyebrows lifted up, but she squeezed his hand back. "I can take whatever you dish out," he said.

She grinned and leaned back against the headrest. "Have I told you yet today how glad I am that you're here?"

"Nope." Harrison was glad that he was here too. He didn't mind crunching numbers, but being with Grace and not being stuck in an office were both immensely better options. It was the choice between playing in a game or running sprints. He'd run the sprints because he knew it would make him faster, but he'd much rather be sprinting in the game.

They chatted about memories from college as they drove to the lawyer's office. It was interesting how differently she perceived Auburn U. They'd both worked hard, but she hadn't been surrounded by student athletes, student officers, and school sponsors like he had.

When they walked into the plush office twenty minutes later, Harrison held out a little hope that the lawyer could help Grace restructure her annuities, but that hope dissipated quickly. The man wasn't at all pompous or a "shyster" like Henry Goodman had claimed. He was down to earth and explained everything in layman's terms. He went so far as to ask his partner to come in and see if there was any way they could restructure things to help ease Grace's financial burden, but the will was ironclad. A half hour later, even though the men had been gracious and kind, Grace walked out with her head slightly bowed like she'd been chastised by the principal.

The bright sunlight washed over them as they stepped onto the sidewalk, and Harrison drew in a breath of humid air. The news they'd received wasn't what either of them wanted to hear, but at least the lawyer appeared to be in Grace's corner. He hated to see Grace looking so down and wanted to restore her smile.

"Where to?" he asked brightly.

Grace turned and stared at him. "Were we in the same meeting?"

Harrison took a long breath. "I know things don't look great right now, but ..." There really wasn't a but. Grace needed to sell or get married. She couldn't keep going like she was.

"It's a lost cause," she filled in for him. "I either sell, get married, or somehow survive on two thousand dollars a month until I turn thirty." She wrapped her arms around herself. "I could survive on that easily if I would've had time to finish school and get a good-paying job, but I'll never survive on it trying to fix that money pit up, and I'll never get my kiddos."

Harrison met her gaze, willing her to find her strength and feistiness again. If she needed a moment to despair, that was fine, but he wanted to be here for her. "You know, I've never seen down-town Mobile, and also I'm starving," he declared.

Grace's brow pinched as she stared him down. Then she shook her head and a small laugh escaped. "Is this you not letting me get discouraged or be a whiny woman?"

"Not get discouraged," Harrison said. "You're the least whiny

woman I've ever met—almost as tough as my mama and sister."
He winked.

"Well, thank you. I like being grouped with your mama and
sister. Hmm. I guess if you've never been to Mobile you have to
walk down Dauphin Street, and then maybe we can find you
some food."

"Sounds great." Harrison couldn't resist putting his arm
around her. "We'll figure the rest out. Trust me." He didn't know
what there was to figure out, but he hated to see her get down
like this.

She glanced up at him with those beautiful blue eyes.
Harrison placed a soft kiss on her forehead, surprising himself
with his boldness.

Grace didn't respond to his comment or the kiss, simply stared
at him for half a beat, then started walking. "This way." But she
stayed close and he kept his arm around her, so Harrison really
hoped she was trusting him. He hoped even more that he could
somehow help her.

———

TRUST ME, TRUST ME. THOSE WORDS REVERBERATED THROUGH HER
brain as she strolled with Harrison down the famous Dauphin
Street. She'd seen the historic brick and painted buildings with
the wrought iron second-story porch facades many times, but it
was relaxing to walk along with Harrison, especially with his arm
around her and his words giving her hope. She didn't know how
they were going to figure anything out, but she wanted to trust him
and trust that the good Lord would help her.

She saw the bar and restaurant Kazoola up ahead and steered
Harrison that way. "You really hungry?"

"Always."

"Oh, good, you'll love this place."

Kazoola looked teeny from the outside and wasn't anything fancy on the inside—wrought iron tables and chairs with a large bar. It was good Southern cooking, friendly staff, and often they'd have entertainment that she enjoyed. They sat down and the voluptuous waitress was quick to take their orders. She kept doing double takes at Harrison, which Grace found kind of funny since the lady was probably in her forties and Harrison didn't seem to notice her significant glances.

"Do you like live entertainment?" Grace asked. A beautiful black lady was warming up in the corner and Grace hoped her voice was as pretty as the rest of her.

"Sure." He said it like *shore*, all drawled out and cute.

Grace smiled at him. "The music helps me forget ..." She trailed off and concentrated on the singer, who had started singing in a low, soulful voice that touched Grace. As the words registered, something about "walking the trail alone, only the good Lord by my side," a tear crested her eyelashes and trailed down her cheek.

Harrison scooted his chair closer to hers. He didn't touch her, but just his solid presence helped. "You're not alone anymore, remember?" His husky voice went down deeper than the singer's words.

Grace looked up at him. Did he understood how horribly she hated being alone? How had he come to her right when she needed him? "Thank you," she managed to whisper for lack of anything witty or significant to say.

Harrison grinned, and those lips of his tempted her like she'd never been tempted in her life. Why did they have to be so full and perfect? Would they be as firm as the rest of him, but soft and yielding to only her? She had no control as she leaned a little closer.

"And an iced tea for the lady and strawberry lemonade for my man here." The waitress with spiky blonde hair and a very daring neckline set their drinks down. "We've been placing bets in the back." Her tongue trailed along her upper lip. "Pray tell, are you Harrison Jackson?"

Harrison leaned back in his chair and gave her a generous smile. "Yes, ma'am, I am."

"Well, I'll be. I'm a huge Auburn fan. Huge! Wait till I tell Tim." She paused and smiled. "The cook. This is a great day. Harrison Jackson is in the house." She grinned at Grace like they shared the same treasure. "I'll be right back with your food, darlin'."

The interruption wasn't timely, but she didn't mind other people fawning over Harrison. He wasn't cocky at all and Grace thought he deserved a lot more praise. "See, I'm not the only one who followed your every game."

"But you're my favorite fan." He winked.

Grace's stomach filled up with warm bubbles and she leaned in close to him again. Harrison stared at her with those beautiful brown eyes. He rested his arm on the back of her chair, slowly closing the distance between them. Grace could hardly stand the suspense and couldn't have cared less that they were in a public place, not when she was about to share the best kiss of her life. Her mama would've been appalled, saying she had no class and wasn't living up to her name. "Grace is all things beautiful, kindly, proper, and saintly," her mama had always said.

Grace focused on Harrison's eyes and let all social propriety fly out the door.

"Food's up." The happy voice interrupted them again.

Grace pulled back, blushing furiously and feeling more than a little put out with their waitress.

"That's fried shrimp and the mac 'n' cheese for the lady, and chicken, waffles, and the best fries in Mobile for my favorite cornerback." She winked broadly, setting their plates down, leaning close to Harrison, and brushing her well-endowed chest cross his arm.

Harrison drew closer to Grace, but smiled kindly at the lady.

"Can I trouble you for an autograph?" the waitress asked.

"Um, sure." Harrison lifted his shoulders at Grace as the waitress dashed back to the kitchen for a paper and pen. She returned quickly, fawning over Harrison while he signed the paper.

Grace threw good manners in the trash, ignoring Harrison and the waitress and plunging her fork into her steaming mac 'n' cheese. The bite was hot but absolutely perfect, with the cheese all melty in her mouth and just the right amount of grease, spice, and bread crumbs. The waitress was still talking about Harrison's stats and future plans, "disappointed as a wolf in an empty henhouse" when she heard he wasn't going on to play professionally. Grace tried one of the fried shrimp and savored the crunchy goodness, ignoring the waitress's tinkling laughter. A fan was one thing; a forty-something lady hitting on her boyfriend was another.

The shrimp caught in her throat. Had she just thought of Harrison as her boyfriend?

"Since your date is ignoring you, beautiful, do you want to dance?" a male voice asked next to Grace.

Grace looked up in surprise at the slicked-back blond hair and good-looking face. "Beau?"

He held out his hand, grinning at her. Grace glanced over at Harrison, who was now ignoring the waitress and watching her closely.

"Dance with me, pretty girl," Beau begged. When Grace didn't respond, he wrapped his hand around her elbow and pulled her to her feet. "I *said*, dance with me."

Harrison slipped past the waitress and was between her and

Beau quicker than a frog could hop out of boiling oil. "Leave her alone," Harrison commanded, low and threatening.

Beau rammed both of his fists into Harrison's chest, which Grace thought was very brave and very stupid, considering Harrison had him by four or five inches and probably eighty pounds. Harrison didn't budge, but simply grabbed Beau's wrist and squeezed it. Beau winced and tried to pull free, but couldn't.

"What are you doing with *him?*" Beau yelled out in frustration. "You're meant for me! From the time we were babies, you've been meant for me."

The music screeched to a stop and the twenty or so patrons in the restaurant stared at them. Grace could've wilted into the floor and been thrilled. "You're drunk," she told him, scraping together the remains of her dignity. "Go on home and stop humiliatin' yourself."

"I'm not drunk enough to put up with seeing you with this loser!" Beau screamed.

Harrison must've put more pressure on Beau's wrist because he cried out, but not nearly as loud as their waitress hollered, "You see here, mister, you got no right to be talkin' to Harrison Jackson like that." She came up in Beau's face and started pushing at him with that overly large front end. Grace's estimation of the lady went up several notches.

"What are you gonna do about it?" Beau winced again, and Grace could've sworn she heard his bones crack.

"You get on out of here," Harrison said quietly, but Grace was certain everyone in the restaurant heard it. "And you never disrespect Grace again or I'll break your wrist right here and now."

The waitress puffed out her chest and harrumphed. Beau and Harrison glared at each other. Within seconds Beau looked away, and Harrison released him. Beau backed off to a safe distance and shouted, "This ain't over, Gracie Lee. You're mine!"

Harrison leapt in Beau's direction. Beau squealed and bolted out of the restaurant like a cottonmouth snake had him in his sights. Harrison stopped at the door, watching him go, then returned to Grace with smooth, even strides.

The waitress cackled. "Good job, Harrison, you scared 'em good." She grinned at the two of them. "Now ..." Her voice got soothing like a sweet mama. "You two kids just forget about that piece o' trash and enjoy your dinner. The tab's on me." She patted Harrison's cheek like a fond aunt. "Haven't seen someone move that fast since you intercepted Ole Miss's quarterback last October." She raised her voice and hollered, "Harrison Jackson is in the house, folks."

The entire restaurant cheered like Harrison had just won the national championship. Grace's face felt hotter than a bowl of grits on the stove. Harrison gave an awkward wave, then got her chair. She settled into it and looked over at him, not sure if she could eat one more bite with the embarrassment rushing through her. To think she'd ever called Beau a friend. He'd been obnoxious at times, but never a complete jerk like that. He was the loser, not Harrison.

"I'm awful sorry," Grace began, grateful when the music started again and the eyes turned away from their table.

"No, you just hush your apologies." Harrison shook his head. "You can't control the way someone else behaves."

Grace inclined her head. She could control who she allowed in her life, though, and she was more than through with Beau. She'd taken care of him for too long and it was time to let him go. Harrison, on the other hand, was very welcome wherever she was. "Thank you for protecting me."

"Anytime." He winked at her and cut a piece of his deep-fried chicken strip perched on a waffle.

Grace tried to follow suit and eat, but nothing tasted as good as it had before, so she simply watched Harrison dive into the meal, offering him one of her shrimp, which he happily took. Their waitress came back to the table a few times, bringing them more drinks and fussing over Harrison. Grace was far from annoyed with the lady now and loved that she'd showcased Harrison for the celebrity that he was.

6

Harrison and Grace drove home in silence. The restaurant scene had made things awkward between them, and that made him far more ticked at Beau than being called a loser had. Harrison might not have been worthy of Grace, but neither was Beau—far from it. How had that idiot found them? Was he following Grace? Mobile wasn't huge, but it was big enough he doubted Beau just spontaneously chose the same restaurant as them. Unless it was a restaurant that Beau and Grace frequented together often.

He noticed he was clenching the steering wheel tight enough to cramp his hand. He released it and shook it out. Grace had been much too quiet and he wanted to draw her out somehow. "Why do you want to adopt children instead of have your own?"

Grace turned to stare at him, and Harrison realized the question was too direct and personal. The silence stretched and scratched as she waited almost a ten count before saying, "I always wanted a brother or a sister, but for some reason my parents didn't agree." She sighed. "So I used to dream about adopting a sibling. Dumb, huh?"

"Not dumb. So your degree is in education so you can work with children?"

"Yes, but I'd rather be a school counselor than a teacher, help those who struggle. During college I was able to volunteer at a child and family support center and I fell in love with the children over and over again, but my heart also got broken repeatedly. There are so many who need a stable family, a home ..." She gestured out the front windshield.

They'd just pulled into her tree-lined driveway. The setting and house were perfect for children to run and play. If Grace could get the house fixed up, maybe she could make it work. Harrison drove slowly up the lane, then put the SUV in park, but he didn't make a move to get out. Maybe it was wrong to encourage her when she had a lot of work ahead, but Grace was determined. If anyone could make it work, she could. "You have a beautiful home to offer them, but I think your love and kindness are even more important."

She gave him a brilliant smile. "Thank you, Harrison. That means a lot." She reached for her door handle.

"Please, let me get it." Harrison jumped out and hurried around to the passenger side door, pulling it open. Grace took the hand he offered and stepped down.

"I will say one thing for you, Harrison Jackson: you sure can move fast."

"Lots of speed training." He kept her hand in his as they sauntered up to the porch. Though the night had taken a bad turn with Beau, he still didn't want it to end. It was beautiful outside, with the cicadas making their quick-tempoed beat and the fireflies winking at them. "Do you want to sit out on the porch a spell?" he asked.

Grace looked up at him so sweetly he almost kissed her right then and there. "I do, but I'm so tired I ache."

Harrison knew what that kind of tired felt like. "No worries. Maybe tomorrow night."

"It's a date."

She unlocked the deadbolt and Harrison swung open the door, then waited for her to lock it again. They walked slowly up the wide staircase together. "So what do we need to work on tomorrow?" he asked.

"Paint, paint, and more paint." She sounded as tired as she said she was.

"Sounds like a party to me." He wasn't great at painting, though, and wondered if he was more hindrance than help.

Grace glanced at him as they reached the top of the stairs and ambled down the hallway. "Why are you really here, Harrison?"

"Pardon me?" They stopped outside her door and he looked down in confusion, but she didn't offer any help. It was like one of the school's sponsors asking him dumb questions like how he was going to change the world through his influence and "the power of the jersey." He was a football player and an accountant, about the only way he could change the world was to be kind like his mama always taught him to be and look out for others. He used to think he would start sports programs to give underprivileged children a chance to excel at the sports they loved like he'd always loved football. Maybe someday, but not today.

He became aware that Grace was waiting for his answer. "Well, I'm here because Mr. Goodman asked me to be." Shoot, that wasn't romantic or kind.

Her eyes widened, then slowly dimmed and shuttered. "That's what I was afraid of." She pulled open her door and slid inside. "Good night. Thank you for being here."

His body could move fast, but his tongue couldn't. She'd closed her door faster than she closed off the emotions playing in her eyes, cutting off their conversation before Harrison could explain that while he'd come because of Mr. Goodman, he would stay forever because of her. Yet she wasn't asking him to stay forever. Just because she'd looked up to him as an athlete didn't mean she actually cared about him as a person.

Grace was focused on getting her house fixed up and her money secured so she could help children. She was noble and beautiful and Harrison wished he would've responded differently to her question. But would it have mattered? He was only here for a short time—the stud Mr. Goodman had sent to fix a problem. Grace didn't really know the real him, and he doubted she ever would.

7

A rock pinged off her window and Grace's eyes flew open. Dang Beau. It was their signal from when they were teenagers and he needed her help, but she had no desire to see him tonight or anytime soon. She stood and strode to the window as another rock hit it. Pushing it open, she called out, "Stop it, Beau!" It was then she noticed the orange glow in his hand, and her heart froze.

"Heya, pretty girl," Beau called out. "Come on down and keep me company." His voice had a singsong quality to it. He was miles past drunk and holding a flaming torch.

She clenched the windowsill with slick fingers. Was he alone, or were his friends with him? He'd run with a rougher and rougher crowd the past few years. "Go home, Beau." She tried to keep her voice a command. Sometimes he listened to her, even when he was drunk, but he could always sense the slightest weakness in her and twist it to his advantage.

She could see his scowl even from the second story. The angry lines in his forehead were outlined by the torchlight. "You come down and make me happy or I'm going to burn your stupid house down," he snarled, looking like an angry badger.

Grace's breath caught and she couldn't respond for several seconds. The awful torch flickered, and though she didn't think he could burn it down completely before she could get some help, she knew this old wood frame would burn quickly and the damage he could cause would be astronomical. He couldn't hurt Sycamore Bay. It was all she had left. Maybe if she got close she could grab the torch or talk some reason into him.

"I-I'm coming," she finally forced out. "Please just wait for me." She backed slowly away from the window, keeping an eye on Beau. Could she talk him down if he was drunk?

Turning away from the window, she heard a loud whoosh and whirled back, terrified of what she might see. A stream of water sprayed from the house hose. She couldn't see who held the hose, but she could see the look of surprise on Beau's face as he and his torch were doused with a rush of water.

"Oh!" Grace cried out, happiness surging through her as the night went dark.

She sprinted out her bedroom door and down the back staircase. Running through the kitchen, she threw on the back porch light. Harrison stood over Beau, who cowered on the ground. She wondered if Harrison had hit him. Beau deserved a thumping with the way he'd been acting lately, but he'd been beat up enough in his life and it hadn't helped him act any better. She'd be surprised if Harrison had hit him; it didn't really fit the easygoing man she'd gotten to know the past few days.

Grace ran to Harrison's side. He had his arms folded over his muscular chest. He glanced at Grace as she approached and nodded to her, then glared down at Beau once more. "Shall we repeat it again?" Harrison asked.

Beau glared at him. "I will never threaten Grace or her home again."

Harrison looked at Grace. "Are you convinced?"

"Not really." But she couldn't stop smiling.

"Go get your phone and call the police, please," Harrison said evenly.

Beau scrambled to his feet. "No! Come on, man." He splayed his hands and begged, looking like a wet weasel. "I was just trying to get a little play with my girl. Don't call the police. My dad will cut me off."

"Guess the water sobered him up a little bit," Grace said to Harrison. What gave Beau the impression she was "his girl"? She'd always been there for him like a friend or sister, but they weren't and never would be romantically involved, no matter how much he thought they were.

Harrison gave her his easy smile, which she was already coming to love. "The water helped a little bit, but I think he's too dim-witted to understand what I'm telling him."

Beau's face flashed resentment and anger, but he smoothed it out quick and stayed focused on Harrison. "Honestly. I'll leave her alone. Don't call the police."

"You know him better than me, Grace. Will he keep his word and leave you alone? If you don't believe him, we need to report the trespassing and the threat so if something happens again it's on his record."

Beau looked at her with pleading eyes. "Please, Gracie Lee. You know me." He swallowed hard. "I drank a lot tonight, but you know I'd never hurt you. I just want to be with you, baby."

Grace folded her arms across her chest, imitating Harrison's standoffish stance, wishing she was strong and threatening like Harrison. "Well, you've blown any chance of that with your stupid tricks."

"I'm sorry, pretty girl. I can just be your friend if that's what you need right now."

Beau's simpering wasn't what convinced her; rather, she remembered their lifelong friendship and that she was so used to protecting him she didn't know how to stop. She'd always been the one to take care of him when he did stupid stuff, and she tried to keep him out of trouble with his daddy. When his daddy thumped him, she'd been the one to nurse him and care for him.

She nodded to Harrison, even though she didn't feel a hundred percent confident. Yet she'd never forget the day Beau had played a simple prank at a pep rally and called the other team's starting lineup, "A bunch of horse dung." The entire student body had roared their approval, but a call from the principal and Beau had barely made it to her house that night. She'd gone to the sheriff after that one, despite Beau's protests, nothing happened but Beau being hit more regularly.

"He'll honor his word," she told Harrison. "If he doesn't, his daddy will beat him better than you just did." She felt a little bad for revealing Beau's family secrets, but Harrison had to understand why she wasn't calling the cops.

Harrison nodded his understanding. "Wish I could say you missed the beating, but he cowered when I came within five feet of him."

Grace was grateful Harrison hadn't resorted to hitting Beau. Though he deserved it this time, she'd always hated seeing him hurt. She turned to Beau. "I don't want to see you again. Get off my property."

Beau's eyes flashed, but he said quietly, "I'm sorry." He put his hands up and backed away, eyeing Harrison nervously. As soon as he was far enough away, he turned and ran.

They watched him go, then as one turned and faced each

other. Grace shifted her weight to her left foot, the grass cool underneath her toes. "Thank you, and ... I'm sorry."

Harrison smirked. "What are you sorry about?"

"I used to call him a friend." She jammed a thumb at the spot Beau had disappeared.

"We all make mistakes." Harrison gave her his slow grin, but then his face grew serious. "Are you all right?"

"How could I not be with you here?"

Harrison smiled, but there was something off, awkward in the air between them. She wished she could pull the words back. Harrison had only come because his boss had asked him to, and she was making it uncomfortable, being so needy and throwing herself at him.

"Thank you," she said quickly before he could respond to her earlier comment. "I'm going to head to bed. Lots to do in the morning."

He nodded, his eyes sober and without their usual warmth as he looked at her. "I'm just going to make sure everything's secure; then I'll come through the back and lock up."

"Okay, thank you again." She scampered away, spinning around on the back porch to search the darkness for him. She couldn't see him and wondered if she'd just made a huge mistake. She should've kissed him in gratitude and worried about how she shouldn't be throwing herself at him later.

She walked slowly up the back staircase and lay on top of her sheets, the comforter thrown to the end of the bed. The June heat didn't abate no matter the time of day or night.

Through the open windows she heard Harrison's phone ring. It was after eleven, quiet enough that his side of the conversation came through if she lay completely still and listened quietly.

"It's all right, sir. I'm sorry Mrs. Goodman hasn't been sleeping well. How is she otherwise?"

Grace slid out of bed and crept to the window, straining to not miss a word. Was this the first time Henry had called him?

"Oh, good, good. Yes, sir—I mean, Henry. Grace is doing all right. She's a mighty brave lady."

Grace flushed at that.

"There's not much to be done about the will, but her old boyfriend's been lurking around." Pause. "Yes, Beau, that's right. I'll stay as long as she needs me to help her." There was another, longer pause. "It's all right, sir. You've been more than generous."

Grace tried to swallow past her dry throat. Of course Henry had offered Harrison some incentive to come help her. Why did that make her feel so small and undesirable?

"Yes, I miss home, but I'm okay. I'll stay for you, sir."

Grace slunk back to bed. She'd heard plenty. Harrison had been so kind to her, but he'd basically said he wished he wasn't here. He wanted to be home and he was only staying for Henry and whatever Henry had promised him. She didn't even know Harrison that well, but he'd become so much more than a football hero to her in a short time. Was it complete selfishness that she didn't want him to leave and she wanted to be more to him than a paycheck?

Turning to her side, she punched her pillow. She'd been silly, assuming Harrison being here meant she wasn't alone anymore. Alone was all she'd ever be.

8

Harrison finished taping off the long baseboard and then tried to paint along the tape with the light blue paint and not have it bleed over onto the white. Things had been a little strained between him and Grace today. He was sure it was his fault for not making some romantic speech after Beau left, but he didn't know what to say to make it better now. He'd had glorious visions last night as Beau cowered before him, and he realized he'd saved Grace's beloved house, that she would fall into his arms, maybe cry a little bit, for sure kiss him a lot. No such luck.

He kept getting the impression that she didn't like his reason for being here, but that made no sense. He wouldn't have even known her or that she needed him without Henry Goodman forcing him here. How was he supposed to change that? He wished he was more accomplished in understanding women. Knowing Grace was outside watering her flowers, he pulled his phone out and hit the contact for his sister, Moriah.

"Hey there, little bro. How's my stuffy accountant?"

Harrison chuckled and swiped more paint on, the heat making his fingers sweaty and not helping his precision at all. "I'm actually painting a house in Mobile, and I need your advice."

"You need my advice on painting? You're horrible at it, quit now."

"I know. But I need your advice on women."

"Oh, gotcha. I'm a much better advisor on that subject for sure. Stop it, Turk ... Jace, keep your hands to yourself! Yes ... okay." She exhaled loudly, but there was laughter in her voice. "Turk and Jace say hey, and you *have* to come visit this weekend."

Oh man, how he would love to go visit them in Montgomery and not just because they had air conditioning. "I wish I could, but I don't think I can leave Grace." And he knew he couldn't pry her away from this house for the weekend.

"Is Grace the women trouble?"

"Yes, ma'am."

"And you're painting her house?"

"It's a long story, but I'm here for work." He kept dragging paint along the baseboard as he talked, glancing out the window every so often. Grace was out in the vegetable garden now. She bent low to pick a pepper, and the air whooshed out of him. Her shape was perfect to him and he could watch her all day long.

He spilled his story to Moriah quickly before Grace came back in. "Grace is amazing and beautiful, but she's acting like a woman. I'm not sure if she's upset because her old boyfriend's coming around causing trouble, or upset because my boss assigned me to be here."

"Okay. First of all, child, don't ever dare say 'she's acting like a woman' to me again or I'll track you down wherever you are and smack you. Second of all, no woman could resist you, little brother. Turn on that Southern 'I'm the football hero of the world' charm."

Harrison smiled, shaking his head. "Sis, you're the only one who thinks no woman can resist me." He didn't have any Southern or football charm. He was just him, who obviously said dumb things like, "she's acting like a woman."

"Oh, brother." He could just imagine the look of despair on her face. "The humility is probably endearing to the women, but it doesn't fly with me. You're a stud muffin!"

"Okay, you calling me a stud muffin is more than a little awkward."

Moriah's deep laugh rang out on the phone. Harrison set the paintbrush down and simply watched Grace pick vegetables and put them in her basket.

"You're the complete package, Harrison. I'm just saying any woman would be nuts not to go for you. The humility is good, but I need you to up the confidence a bit, all right? Throw those burly shoulders back, put a smile on that handsome mug, talk to her so she can know the genuine, kind man you are, and she'll be chasing after you faster than Turk can eat a candy bar."

Harrison knew exactly why he'd called Moriah. He needed this dose of confidence, even if she was more than a little biased. He watched as Grace walked toward the house, then swiped the sweat off his forehead with the back of his hand and picked up his paintbrush again. "Thanks, sis. I'll try my best."

"Get your bum up here and visit us. Bring Grace, and we'll make sure she's head over heels for you before you leave."

He laughed, not sure if time spent with Moriah would draw Grace in or terrify her. He adored his sister, but she could be a little overwhelming to some people. He smiled. Grace could hold her own with anyone, and she'd probably love Moriah. "I'll see if I can make it work."

"That's a no." Moriah sighed dramatically. "I'll just keep

praying for you, then, and the good Lord will provide. I didn't even ask—is this girl worthy of you?"

"She's an angel." Turning, Harrison drew in a quick breath. Grace stood in the archway of the sitting room, her beautiful mouth slightly open. "I'll talk to you soon, sis."

Her goodbye was shut off as he pushed the end button on the phone and dropped it into his pocket.

Grace set the vegetables down and walked a few steps into the room. "Your sister?" she asked. Then her cheeks turned pink. "Sorry. That's none of my business."

"It's okay. It was my sister."

"Is she close by?"

"Montgomery."

"That's nice." There was so much more in her eyes than nice. Did she realize he'd called *her* an angel? She bent down and checked underneath the tape, gasping slightly. "Oh, Harrison, you really are horrible at this."

Harrison dropped the brush into the paint tray and moved right up close to her. She straightened, and he could smell her heady scent, vanilla and lilacs in the springtime. Her silky hair brushed his cheek. She glanced up at him, and he couldn't care less about painting as her blue eyes with those pretty, long lashes focused in on him.

"I am?" he asked, deep and low.

She swallowed and her gaze darted down to his lips, then back up to his eyes. "At ... painting," she clarified. "I imagine you're right good at everything else."

Harrison lifted an eyebrow and was about ready to try out her lips and hope he was "right good" at kissing. He imagined that if he was kissing her, his skill set wouldn't matter much with the sparks and warmth tracing between them. He leaned down closer and she arched up.

A loud rap at the door made Grace stumble back, hitting her backside on the fresh paint. Harrison cursed whoever was at that door. If it was Beau, he would thump him good this time. He offered Grace a hand. She accepted, and he wanted to rail at the person knocking again. If her hand in his felt this good, what would a kiss be like?

Grace released his hand and rushed around him. Harrison followed. This woman could lead him around like a puppy dog without any kind of leash.

———

GRACE TRIED TO COMPOSE HERSELF AND NOT BE ANGRY AT WHOEVER was pounding on her door, even though they'd just interrupted what she was sure would've been the best kiss of her life. Who cared if Harrison had only come for Henry Goodman? He was here now.

"*She's an angel.*" Harrison had said that to his sister. Was he talking about Grace? She could hope.

Swinging the door wide, her heart immediately softened. Uncle Mike and Aunt Geraldine stood on the porch with a peach pie and ice cream in hand and wide, oh-so-needed smiles on their faces. "There's our girl," Aunt Geraldine squealed, dragging Grace into her arms.

Grace relaxed against Aunt Geraldine's soft frame, missing her mama and basking in the comfort of her lifelong adopted aunt. Aunt Geraldine released her and she got a one-armed hug from Uncle Mike, who was trying to balance the ice cream and pie that smelled wonderfully of warm crust, fresh peaches, and sugar.

"Well, who is *this* handsome man?" Aunt Geraldine said coyly.

Grace turned to see Harrison reclining against the doorjamb— his dark eyes smoldering at her and those perfect lips turned up in a smile. Had she really almost kissed those lips? She felt a little faint just thinking about it. Handsome honestly didn't do him justice. "This is my ... friend, Harrison Jackson. Henry Goodman sent him here to help me."

Uncle Mike stuck his hand out, but a look of frustration traced across his black eyes. "Any friend of Henry's is a friend of ours," he said.

Grace didn't understand why Uncle Mike had seemed upset for a second. His and Aunt Geraldine's daughter had married a white man and they had been thrilled. He couldn't possibly be upset that Grace was wanting to be in a biracial relationship. Then it hit her. He probably thought she and Harrison were being immoral, spending night and day in this house together. Her cheeks got hot, but she didn't know how to explain.

Harrison stepped onto the porch and shook his hand. "Thank you, sir."

"Mike and Geraldine Huesser," Uncle Mike said, releasing his hand.

Aunt Geraldine wrapped her arms around Harrison's waist. It made Grace smile to see her rounded aunt with the tall, strong Harrison. "Are you here to help our girl?" Aunt Geraldine asked.

"Yes, ma'am."

She released him and glanced up at Uncle Mike, who fixed Harrison with a stern look. "Grace's daddy was my best friend," he said. "And this little girl is like one of my own. You treat her right, you hear?"

"Yes, sir." Harrison shifted from foot to foot. Grace had never seen him this uncomfortable. "I promise I will, sir."

Uncle Mike locked eyes with Harrison for a few seconds, then finally nodded.

"Whew." Aunt Geraldine fanned her face. "Looks like you passed muster." She giggled and gestured them all inside. "Well, let's get in the kitchen and eat this delicacy. Baked it myself, so I know it's going to be heavenly." She winked at Harrison.

Harrison chuckled, and Aunt Geraldine's reference to heaven made Grace think of Harrison saying she was an angel. She didn't care that Harrison had leaked blue paint onto the white baseboards. This day was looking to be her best in a long while.

9

Harrison really liked Grace's adopted aunt and uncle, especially the endearing Aunt Geraldine. They enjoyed a nice visit about Mike and Geraldine's recent travels to the cool beauty of Maine, and discussed Harrison's football career. Together, they walked them out to the porch after enjoying the delicious pie and ice cream.

Uncle Mike pulled Grace aside and said in a low tone, "Honey, I think you should really consider selling this place." When Grace's mouth tightened, he lifted his hands. "I know how you love it here and the connection with your mama and daddy, but sweetheart, it's too much. Come stay with us, finish your school-ing, have a life." He tapped her nose. "You need to think of your-self once in awhile."

Grace sighed and gave him a hug, stretching up on her tiptoes to kiss his cheek. "I'll think about it."

"Okay. Love you, little girl. We can come by anytime you need us." He squeezed her tight, then offered his arm to Aunt Geraldine.

Aunt Geraldine gave Grace a long hug and Harrison a quick one, muttering, "You take care of my princess, you hear me boy?"

Harrison grinned. "Yes, ma'am. It's my first priority."

"It'd better be." She swatted him on the rear before taking her husband's arm and sauntering away.

Harrison chuckled. He stood next to Grace, watching their Maxima pull away. Had the past hour changed things between them? A guy could hope, but her eyes were as shuttered as ever and her arms were folded tightly across her chest. Uncle Mike's parting words were obviously not what she wanted to hear.

Grace pushed out a long breath and muttered, "We'd better get back to work. Do you mind going to the shed and grabbing the white trim paint?"

Harrison's neck got warm. "Sure. Sorry I messed the paint up."

She laughed at that. "Should make you redo it, but I don't think it would help."

He grinned. "No, probably not."

Her smile fled. "Thanks for being here, Harrison ... and not giving me unsolicited advice." She scowled in the direction Uncle Mike and Aunt Geraldine had left.

"He's just trying to help the only way he knows how." Harrison wasn't sure why he was defending Uncle Mike's words, but he sort of agreed with him. The will was locked, and this property was too big for Grace to maintain. Harrison had told her he'd stay until they figured it out, but he didn't see any solution, besides selling, that would put an end to her indentured service to this house. Her parents were gone and that was tough, but at some point she'd have to let the past go and find herself a future.

Luckily he didn't voice any of this, as the little bit he did say brought fire to her eyes. "I'll go get the white paint," she said.

Harrison reached out a hand. Things had been better since she'd heard him tell Moriah she was an angel, and here he'd gone and messed it up again. How he missed the simple life of football and school. "No, I've got it."

Hurrying off the porch, he stomped around the house and to the shed. Why didn't she listen to sense? Beautiful, smart, fun, and so stinking frustrating. He flung open the shed door and his eyes adjusted slowly to the darkness. It reeked of gasoline. Had he spilled when he filled up the lawn mower? It wouldn't still stink from two days ago.

Whew. It was so strong he got an instant headache. *Get the paint and get out quick.* He remembered putting the white paint on the top shelf to the right yesterday. He felt his way that direction, but stumbled over something big and plastic. There hadn't been anything on the floor last time he was in here. Pulling his phone out, he clicked on his flashlight and shone it down. His eyes widened and the air rushed out of him. The entire floor of the shed was covered with red five-gallon gas cans. These hadn't been here yesterday. Pushing at a few of them, he confirmed they were full, and the smell told him it was definitely gas.

He rushed back out of the shed and bumped into Grace. Grasping her elbows, he kept her from falling into the grass.

"Harrison?" she questioned. "Are you okay?"

He shook his head and directed her back to the shed. "Look." He shone his flashlight around the shed.

Grace gasped. "Who put these here?"

"I have no idea, but we need to call the police."

"Beau?" she wondered.

He hoped not. Even though the kid was a punk, he knew it would hurt Grace to have it be her old friend. They stepped out of the shed and into the bright sun, trying to clear their noses and heads of the acrid smell of gasoline.

Before he could dial 911, Grace turned to him, her blue eyes bright with unshed tears. "Maybe Uncle Mike's right and I need to sell. Someone obviously wants to scare me to death, burn my house down, kill me, or a combination of all three. If they're trying to scare me, they're rock stars at it. I can't take care of this place by myself and you've got to get back to your real life sometime." She blinked, and the tears spilled over her dark lashes and down her smooth cheeks. Her blue eyes were so bright and lovely he wanted to make everything better for her.

Harrison wrapped her small frame in his arms. "We'll figure it out," he murmured. "I'm not leaving until we do. I think they're just trying to scare you, or why would they leave these where they knew we'd find them? If you decide to sell, it will be because *you* want to, not because someone is trying to scare you away."

"Oh, Harrison." She kind of choked on his name, like she was full to the brim with emotion.

Grace circled her arms around his back and cuddled in closer against him. Harrison savored her sweet, clean smell, and how perfectly she fit in his arms. For the hundredth time, he wanted to kiss her and never stop, but this obviously wasn't the right moment. Maybe after the police left and hopefully figured out who would stack an old wooden shed with gas cans.

Harrison suddenly felt beat down and hated how out of his control all of this was. He wasn't sure he wanted to face another day of the uncertainty and odd things that were happening. He wasn't sure how Grace was holding up as well as she was. He'd been a college athlete, but he'd never been as exhausted as he was right now. Still, it was worth it to be here and hold her like this.

GRACE TOSSED AND TURNED FOR WHAT FELT LIKE HOURS. THE POLICE had taken fingerprints from the shed and the gas cans and then removed all the gas cans to keep them safe, promising to drive by as often as they could. She had told the police about Beau threatening her the other night. She hated to think Beau would really try to burn her house down, but he'd changed so much the past couple of years that she hardly knew him anymore.

Sadly, she couldn't afford any kind of security or help ... besides Harrison. She cuddled deeper into her sheets, remembering being in his arms. He didn't smell like some expensive cologne like Beau, but like clean, mouthwatering man. She wished she could've kept hugging him all day and all night.

A soft bang came from downstairs. Grace sat upright, clinging to the sheet. Had someone broken into the house? She'd been concerned about safety before today, but to see all those gas cans and have it confirmed that someone wanted to hurt her, her house, or both of them had really pushed her over the edge. Sliding open the drawer next to her nightstand, she pulled out her gun, comforted by the cool metal in her hand. She grabbed her phone in her other hand and hurried out the door and to Harrison's room.

Footsteps came from downstairs, she guessed the kitchen. Her spine prickled and she didn't dare alert the intruder by knocking on Harrison's door. She quietly turned the knob and slipped inside.

"Harrison?" she whispered.

No response.

Tiptoeing to his bed, she saw the comforter was turned down and the sheets were mussed, but he wasn't in there. She hurried back out of his room, checking the bathroom on her way to the stairs, empty as well. Hopefully it was just Harrison downstairs, but she wasn't taking any chances as she gripped the gun and quietly made her way down the back staircase to the kitchen. A soft light filtered up the stairs from the kitchen. Her hands were clammy. She reached for the railing with her left hand and dropped her phone. It clunked down several stairs. Grace bit at her tongue, grimacing. If an intruder was here, she'd just announced her whereabouts like an innocent woman walking south of I-10 at night. No mistaking that she was here and could easily be attacked.

She hurried down the steps as quietly as she could and picked up her phone. The kitchen light turned off, and she gasped. Whoever was down there had heard her and was most likely preparing to do her harm. Should she turn around? Call out for Harrison? Call the police?

Soft, cautious footsteps padded toward the stairs. Grace froze, not daring to retreat or proceed. Saying a silent prayer for help, she fumbled with the gun and the phone, but managed to get the flashlight turned on and swung it into what she hoped was the intruder's eyes. "Get out of here or I'll shoot first and then call the police to clean up your lazy carcass!" she hollered, loud as her papa would've yelled if someone had been on his bad side.

"Grace!" Harrison's voice floated up to her. "It's me."

"Oh, thank heavens." Grace released her tight grip on the revolver as the light in the kitchen was switched back on. The oxygen swept out of her and she felt weak and relieved. She descended the stairs on wobbly legs. Harrison waited for her, concern written all over his handsome face. He didn't say anything, but took her elbow and led her to the table, where the rest of the peach pie sat beckoning in its tin. Pulling out a seat, he waited until she sat, then gently pushed the chair back in close to the table.

"Thank you," Grace murmured. She laid the gun and her phone on the butcher-block table and clenched her still-trembling hands together.

"Sorry if I scared you, turning off the light like that," he said. "I didn't want to be a sitting duck if it was someone besides you."

"I reacted the same way, praying it was you, but scared that it wasn't."

A long pause ensued before Harrison asked, "Pie?"

"You were hoping just to eat it all yourself," she tried to tease, but it still came out shaky.

Harrison grinned. "I was thinking about it." He got another plate, cut her a generous piece, and put it on the plate. "Ice cream?"

"No, this is fine." But Grace didn't pick up the fork he'd set next to her plate.

"I couldn't sleep," Harrison admitted, cutting a large bite of his slice of pie and putting it in his mouth. She loved him for giving her a second to calm down and not addressing how nuts she'd just acted.

Grace watched him chew and swallow, fascinated by the way his mouth moved in rhythm, then how his throat bobbed as he swallowed. She'd never met a man whose movements were so smooth and refined like Harrison—from the football field to escorting her around to eating pie. She'd never been as attracted to or intrigued by a man. Maybe it was also because Harrison was one hundred percent man. He wasn't an immature boy like Beau or many of the other guys she'd dated in high school and college.

She tried to pick up her fork to take a bite of her pie, but her hand was still shaking too much. She quickly released the fork onto the table with a soft clunk. "I couldn't sleep either," she admitted.

"I'm sorry I scared you," he said.

"Wasn't your fault." She stared at the pie, but the thought of food turned her stomach. Pushing the plate away, she clasped her hands together under the table. "It's hard to believe someone wants to burn me and my house down." A tear crested her lid and rolled down her cheek. She was really so alone in the world, and now someone wanted to hurt her beloved home. Why? How could the good Lord take her Mama and Daddy? Why couldn't Uncle Mike and Aunt Geraldine see how much the house meant to her? They'd lived here for many years and should be fighting for the house more than she was. Yet Uncle Mike couldn't keep this place maintained on his own and he had a lifetime of experience. What made her think she could succeed?

She glanced at Harrison, who studied her like she was a fragile China doll. "Sorry." She brushed the tear away. "I'm not usually an emotional mess."

Harrison set his fork down and licked a pie crumb off his lips. "You don't need to apologize. You have every right to be frustrated and concerned." He glanced at the old burner stove. "But I promise you, Grace, I'm going to be here for you."

Grace wanted to know if he was here for her, or because he'd promised Henry Goodman to be here, but at the moment she didn't care. She just wanted him, wanted him here, wanted all of him—take your pick.

She stared at him until he met her gaze again. When he did, his gaze was full of promise, tenderness, and a sexy smolder that made her stomach erupt into butterflies. Harrison pushed away from the table and stood. With slow, deliberate movements, he kept that warm gaze on her and pulled her chair away from the table also, his hands brushing her arm and her side.

Grace's breath came in short pants. His intentions were pretty clear and she had that impression again of Harrison being all man. Even though he was kind and considerate, he was going to pursue what he wanted: at the moment he wanted her. It was delicious anticipation, wondering exactly how he was going to claim her and how it was going to feel.

Harrison gently grasped her forearm and helped her out of the chair. Grace's knees were weak and knocking together, but for a completely different reason than the fear of a few minutes ago. Harrison turned her to face him and studied her face. Cupping her chin with his large palm, he took a step closer, his muscular frame overshadowing her. His crisp man scent was even stronger tonight.

Grace tilted her head back and waited, her lips parted slightly with anticipation. Harrison bent down, gently pressing his lips to hers. The touch was brief and sweet and satiated her like an ice cube satiated a thirsting man. Those lips were every bit as perfect as she'd imagined.

She flung her arms around his neck, lifted up onto her tiptoes, and drank in the feel of his lips on hers like cool, delectable water. He tasted like peach pie and every good dream she'd ever had.

Harrison may or may not have chuckled at her forward move, but he returned her kiss without hesitation. Lifting her completely off her feet, he swung her around and set her on the edge of the kitchen counter. Boldly running his hands up her back and across her bare shoulders, he took the kiss to the next level of intimacy and deliciousness. She let out a little moan and he smiled against her mouth, then returned to kissing her thoroughly. Grace leaned into his broad chest, happy as punch that he didn't wear a shirt to bed as she explored the defined musculature of his back with her fingertips.

When he finally pulled back, she was feeling decidedly dizzy and was grateful she was sitting down. Cupping her face with both palms, Harrison murmured, "You're beautiful, Grace Lee Addison."

Grace let out a giggle, embarrassed at how girlish it sounded but too happy to care very much. "How'd you know it was Lee?"

Her mama used to call her Grace Lee and Beau called her Gracie Lee, but she didn't use her middle name much.

"Every girl I know has the middle name Lee."

Grace laughed again, but the intimacy of the moment had disappeared. She slid off the counter, brushing against Harrison's chest. He smiled down at her and she wanted to kiss him again, but figured she'd been forward enough for one night.

"I'd better get some rest," she finally said.

"I hope you can sleep now."

"The kissing was a great distraction."

He grinned, and she had to grab the countertop for support. He truly was an exquisite man to look at, but his gentle interior and willingness to help her made him even more attractive.

She turned to go back to bed, filled with warmth, joy, and Harrison's kisses. What would she do if Harrison hadn't come? She reached the stairs, but the thought that wouldn't leave since she'd overheard the phone call with Henry begged an answer, now. Why had he truly come? He was smart, good-looking, hard-working. Why wasn't he at home succeeding in his new career instead of helping some woman he hadn't known until a few days ago? "What did Henry pay you to come help me?"

Harrison leaned back against the counter, folded his defined arms across his chest, and swallowed before answering. "Double my salary and a promise of turning his clients over to me when I return to Montgomery."

"Thank you for being honest."

He studied her but didn't say anything. She really wanted him to say something—claim it wasn't about the money now, reassure her if he'd known her he would've come for nothing. It was silly and so immature of her, and she was reminded once again that he was a man and not the type to fill the air with empty words.

"Night," she whispered, then turned to tread back up the stairs, cursing herself for tainting that kiss with a question about money. Of course Henry offered Harrison something big to get him to leave his home, family, and career and come save the silly damsel in distress. Why did it open a cavity in her chest, achy and oozing, to think that Harrison was only here for the money and that kiss couldn't possibly have meant to him what it meant to her? She didn't know that, but she couldn't shake the feeling.

10

Harrison awoke with a smile on his face, the remembrance of Grace on his lips, and an absolutely brilliant idea. He texted Moriah quick and she agreed it was perfect, but he had to recruit some more help. At breakfast he got the opportunity he needed when Grace ran outside to grab a couple of peaches for them. She'd been on her phone googling paint color ideas for the kitchen, but she left her phone on the counter to go outside and the lock screen hadn't gone back into place. He scrolled through her contacts and placed a quick call to Aunt Geraldine. She readily agreed with his plan and promised they'd be there the next afternoon.

Things seemed comfortable between him and Grace throughout the next day and a half, but she was quiet and neither of them tried to resume the intimacy from their kiss. He kept worrying that she was dwelling on why he'd come here originally, not why he had kissed her. The money was not important to him —she was. But how to tell her that without sounding trite or like he was assuming she wanted him to stay for reasons beyond Henry Goodman and his job?

About four o'clock in the afternoon, he took the paintbrush from her hand and said, "The paint looks great. I need you to go shower and pack an overnight bag."

"Excuse me?" She stared up at him and put a hand on her hip, Southern-girl style. He loved it.

"We're going away for the night."

"Excuse *me*," she said again. A wrinkle creased her forehead. "What kind of girl do you think I am?" The accent was thick and irresistible.

He couldn't resist touching that wrinkle and smiling. They'd been alone the past four days and she hadn't taken exception. "We won't be alone and your beloved Sycamore Bay won't be unattended. C'mon, Grace Lee, let me take you away and forget about your worries and your strifes." He sang the last part.

She laughed then. "I like your deep voice. You'd be perfect for 'The Bare Necessities.'"

"Hey, I'm not quite as big as Baloo."

Her eyes skimmed over his shoulders and chest, and she sighed. "You're big enough."

Harrison barely resisted flexing. "Will you go away with me?"

"Where?" she murmured, looking so kissable and beautiful with her hair in a messy ponytail and a pale blue paint smear on her cheek.

"It's a surprise, but I think you'll like it."

"I can't leave my house." She gestured around. "What if whoever left those gas cans comes back?"

"I talked to the detective again this morning. They're watching the house and Beau closely." The police hadn't found any fingerprints on the gas cans or any proof that Beau was the instigator, but they had been great to take the threat seriously.

"That's right good of them, but I still don't feel as if I can leave the house empty."

He pulled his trump card. "Mike and Geraldine agreed to come stay at the house while we're gone."

"Well, aren't you thoughtful?" She moistened her lips and blinked up at him.

"I try." He spread his hands wide and tried to look innocent and not cocky. What he really wanted to do was kiss her again, but he needed to let her commit to going away first. He knew it would be hard for her to leave her house, but Moriah was a good medicine that everyone needed once in a while. "Please come with me?"

She stared at him for half a beat, then stepped closer, stood on tiptoes, and kissed his cheek. "I'd like that. Thank you, Harrison."

Before he could think of a smooth way to extend the kiss, she spun and strode to the grand staircase. Harrison wanted to chase after her, sweep her off her feet and kiss her in every room of this house, but he refrained. He needed to take this slow, make sure she knew he was here for her and not anything Henry Goodman had promised him. Moriah would help him make that possible and then some.

11

G race sat in Harrison's SUV, watching the trees and large estates sliding by outside the window. It had only taken them two and a half hours to drive to Montgomery. Harrison's hometown. Was he going to take her to meet his mama or sister? Would it be awkward? She still couldn't quite believe he'd recruited Uncle Mike and Aunt Geraldine to come watch the house. Really, it was the only way she wouldn't stress about something happening ... but what if somebody tried to burn it down while she was gone, and they hurt Uncle Mike or Aunt Geraldine? The thought made her shiver.

"You cold?" Harrison reached for the temperature control.

"No." Grace wrapped her fingers around his hand to stop him from changing the air. Awareness crawled through her at even a simple touch of his skin.

Harrison's eyes swept from the road to her face. He turned his hand palm up and interlaced their fingers, then rested them on the console between them. Contented and wondering if she would get the chance to kiss him again soon, she leaned back in her seat with a smile. Harrison hadn't reassured her that he was here for her and not for Henry Goodman, but he was a good, salt-of-the-earth kind of man. He wouldn't play with her emotions if he didn't care about her.

"Why the shiver, then?"

"You notice everything, don't you?"

"Everything about you."

She smiled and squeezed his hand. "I was just worrying, what if something happened to Uncle Mike or Aunt Geraldine while we were gone?"

Harrison nodded his understanding. "The police are taking the threat seriously and promised to drive by often, and Uncle Mike's a tough old guy. I know he gave me a stare down I won't forget." He winked at her. "I don't think anybody would mess with him."

She tilted her head and studied him. "I don't think anyone would mess with you either."

"Ah, I'm like a puppy dog."

She laughed.

Harrison pulled off the road a few minutes later and up a tree-lined drive. The huge oaks and sycamores were beautiful, but nothing she hadn't seen before. The three-story restored mansion with two levels of wraparound porch and pillars took her breath away. It was what she dreamed Sycamore Bay would look like when she got it all fixed up. Okay, her house was only half as big as this place, but it was a similar Civil War–era style. The property was immaculate, flowers bloomed everywhere, and the grass looked professionally trimmed. She thought of Harrison pushing her old hand mower around, and her face heated up. Why had she assumed he hadn't come from money? Why in the world had he really come to help her? His family had to be a lot wealthier than his boss and her dad's good friend, Henry.

Harrison pushed the button to turn the car off and smiled over at her, but quickly sobered. "What's wrong?"

Grace swallowed and whispered, "Why didn't you tell me?"

"Tell you ..." He cocked his head to the side and studied her.

"I'm sorry." She gripped the leather seat under her bare legs. Her floral skirt and silky tank top suddenly seemed very underdressed. "It's dumb. I just assumed you didn't come from money, and I am so confused why you'd come help me, why you'd even be working for an accountant, if this is how you grew up." She flung a hand out the window at the mansion.

Harrison chuckled. "If we have time tomorrow, I'll take you by my parents' house and you'll laugh at what you just said."

"So you're not ... a multimillionaire?"

"Driving a Hyundai?" Harrison squeezed her hand.

The nine-foot wood and etched glass front door of the mansion popped open and a little boy and a beautiful, petite lady with black, curly hair sprinted for the car, both grinning wide. A tall blond man followed them at a more leisurely pace.

"Brace yourself," Harrison said.

Harrison's door was flung open by the lady, but the little boy scurried around his mother and climbed into Harrison's arms before she could reach him. "Uncle Hare, you came, you came!"

Harrison held onto the boy and stood, giving the lady a hug. She squeezed him tight. "Praise the Lord, our little boy's come home!"

Grace frowned in confusion. This woman looked younger than Harrison, but she talked like an eighty-year-old grandma.

Grace's door swung open and she looked up, way up, into the bright blue eyes and wide smile of the blond man. "I know Harrison would want to get your door," he said, "but they'll be mauling him for at least another half an hour."

"Oh, you hush now," the lady said. "I just need a Harrison hug.

Then I'll be fine." She peered through the car at Grace, her dark eyes bright with happy tears. "He gives the best hugs in the world."

Grace couldn't argue with that. She just about told Harrison's sister he gave the best kisses too, but didn't know how that would go over. The man stepped back and gestured her out. Grace climbed onto the cement driveway, the heat radiating over her sandaled toes. The man extended his hand. "Jace Browning, Harrison's brother-in-law and that beautiful lady's husband."

Grace shook his hand, liking this friendly man.

"You'd better be calling it how it is, boy," his wife said, "or you'll get none of my sweetness."

Jace kept grinning at Grace. "The sweetest, most beautiful wife in the world."

"Now don't lay it on too thick, or it doesn't feel genuine anymore." Her accent was strong and Grace loved her immediately.

Harrison steered his sister and nephew around the front of the car to Jace and Grace. "Grace, this is my sister, Moriah; my nephew, Turk; and my brother-in-law, Jace."

Grace smiled at all of them. Moriah released her hold on Harrison and threw her arms around Grace. "You're so very welcome here, honey. I was awful sorry to hear about your daddy."

"Thank you," Grace managed, surprised at the hug and the authentic warmth behind the words.

Moriah pulled back. "Y'all better come in the house and start eating. I've been cooking since Harrison called me yesterday morning."

Grace shot Harrison a look. He shrugged innocently. His nephew looked teeny against his broad chest. The nephew was probably about four or five, and had a full head of dark, curly hair and the cutest rounded cheeks. His skin was a shade lighter than

Harrison's and his deep brown eyes sparkled at Grace. "Mama, I think Harrison's wife is prettier than you."

All the adults choked on their laughter, except for Grace, whose neck and cheeks got so hot she wondered if she was purple.

"Nobody's as pretty as your mama, son," Jace corrected him, opening his arms.

Turk launched from his uncle to his daddy's arms. "I know my mama's the most beautifulest woman in the world, but maybe Grace is just as beautiful. I don't know." He lifted his little shoulders innocently, then gave Grace a suggestive look. "You wanna be my girlfriend, or you gotta be Uncle Hare's wife?"

Grace couldn't help but laugh, no matter how red her face was. "I'm not his wife, so I'd love to be your girlfriend."

"Yes!" Turk pumped his fist in the air, then brought it down to his side.

Moriah had tears streaking her face, she was laughing so hard. "You shoulda seen your face when he said you was Harrison's wife." She shook her head. "Sorry, sweet girl. I don't want to be laughing at my new friend, but that was classic."

They walked slowly up the sidewalk and several sets of stairs bordered with petunias, begonias, and a white ground cover flower that smelled like vanilla, which she figured was clematis. When she could afford more flowers, she would buy some clematis for sure.

"It's okay. At least I got a boyfriend out of the deal." Grace winked at Turk.

Harrison groaned. "I should've known not to bring her around here where Turk would steal her from me."

"*All* the girls love me," Turk said.

The adults laughed again.

"I'm sure they do," Grace said.

Turk pumped his eyebrows.

They made it to the wide front porch with beautiful wood rockers gracing it and what looked to be the original hardwood flooring, stained dark and perfect. The white trim on the railings and beams contrasted beautifully.

"Oh, I love this house so much," Grace couldn't help but say.

"Wait until you get inside." Moriah nodded. It wasn't bragging; Moriah was as enamored with her home as Grace was.

"She promised me if I bought her the house of her dreams, she'd travel with me at least a week a month," Jace explained.

Grace had so many questions pinging around in her head. What did Jace do to be so wealthy he could buy his young wife her dream mansion and travel the world as well? She didn't think it would be polite to drill him with questions, though, and when he pushed open the wood and etched glass front doors and the air conditioned air whooshed over her, all other thoughts disappeared.

This house was flawless: cherry hardwood flooring; a grand staircase that swept up gracefully, then curved both right and left; an open balcony surrounding the second story and more stairs leading to the third; wooden chair railings and crown moldings; antique wooden furniture with live floral arrangements and unreal landscape portraits ... and that was just the entryway.

"Please just let me sit here and soak it in for a few days," Grace murmured.

Moriah gave a deep, throaty laugh. "Sorry, you've got to help me eat some of the food or I'll be as round as my mama."

Grace looked to Harrison for help. "Who can think of food at a time like this?"

Harrison put his arm around her waist and she leaned against him, loving how natural yet exciting it felt. "If I promise to give you a tour of every square inch of the house, will you eat first and not offend my only sibling? Her food is so good I think about it several times a day."

Grace stiffened, as she wasn't certain if Harrison was teasing her or if she really was upsetting Moriah by not wanting to eat her food. "Oh, I'm sorry."

"Go on." Moriah pushed a hand at her. "I think you're a doll for loving my house. We'll eat quick; you've seen how this boy can put it away."

Grace walked with Harrison, sneaking peeks at the office off the right of the entry with a massive walnut desk and bookcases, and a formal music room on the left with a grand piano, harp, and a drum set. She could just imagine the damage Turk could do to everyone's eardrums with that. They entered a dining room beyond the music room. A long, oval table sat majestically in the middle of the room, more fresh flowers gracing the center with a display of Lladro china on the walnut hutch to her right. A sideboard with antique hot plates was filled to capacity. The yeasty scent of homemade rolls competed with the roast. She was brought back to Sunday dinners with her mama, daddy, Uncle Mike, Aunt Geraldine and their two girls.

Everything looked as good as it smelled and she felt guilty for not wanting to eat first, but she could hardly wait to tour every room of the house. She contented herself with taking in the details of the dining room, the creamy walls and oak trim, the large windows overlooking a stretch of grass and the sycamore trees beyond. Harrison was unbelievably thoughtful to rescue her from working on her house nonstop and give her a mini-vacation in a place that was paradise to her.

———

HARRISON FELL HARDER FOR GRACE EVERY MOMENT HE SPENT WITH

her. Turk was right in that she was the most beautifulest woman in the world, but her intelligence, her wit, her passion for football and Southern houses, and the way he felt when he touched and kissed her—not to mention a thousand other little details that were solely Grace—had him wrapped up like a football in a running back's arms.

She made a fuss over Moriah's roast and potato dinner, especially the rolls and pecan pie, which were delectable. Baking was Moriah's specialty; she used to bake every day for her friend Trin's bed and breakfast before she met Jace.

Throughout the tour of the house after dinner, Grace and Moriah became instant best friends. After the tour, Turk begged Grace to swim with him in the pool. She swam like she was born in the water, and her tanned legs and arms looked perfect to him in her one-piece suit. Too many times she caught him staring at her, and sometimes he caught her staring at him.

They swam until dark and then went to their own suites to shower. Though this home was built in the mid-1800s, the mansion had been remodeled so most of the suites on the second and third floors had their own private bathrooms.

Harrison showered quickly but had no desire to go to bed. He crept out of his room into the third-story hallway. Grace's room was just two doors down. Maybe he could ask if she wanted to go listen to the cicadas in the backyard ... or was that just code for "I want to kiss you in the dark"?

He could hear Moriah's voice floating up from the open balcony of the second floor, arguing with Turk about going to bed, promising he'd see Grace in the morning. Turk protested even more loudly. Jace's low rumble soothed them both.

Harrison smiled. He wanted that someday, though Grace wasn't close to as feisty as Moriah. He stopped outside Grace's bedroom door and paused. He actually wanted it right now, with

Grace. The breath popped out of his lungs and he had to lean against the wall. That was insane thinking. He hadn't known her a week yet. But he couldn't lie to himself: Grace consumed his every thought. He'd never dreamed of bringing a girl to meet his sister before. Watching the two of them together, seeing Grace fall under Turk's spell of adorableness, exchanging smiles over all of their heads with Jace ... it'd been perfect. He wanted it. No, he *needed* it.

He rapped softly on the door. "Grace?"

The door popped open. She stood there in a tank top, cut-off yoga pants, no makeup, and her blonde hair wet and darker.

"You are so beautiful," he managed to get out.

She grabbed his T-shirt, tugged him inside the room, and shut the door. Harrison stood there, powerless. He'd dominated some of the toughest football players in the nation, but this woman had complete control over him. She pushed at his chest and backed him against the wall.

"What were you hoping to accomplish coming into my room like this?" She elevated an eyebrow, her blue eyes laughing at him.

"Well, ma'am." He tried to sound suave or cool or something, but he was complete putty. "Just a little ole goodnight kiss."

She elevated one eyebrow.

"If that's too much to ask for," he hurried to say, "I'd settle for a hug."

Grace took a step closer and her body brushed his, setting off a smolder in the pit of his stomach. He was gulping air like he'd just run sprints. She arched onto tiptoes, bracing herself against him with her hands on his chest. Harrison let out a decidedly unmanly moan. The linemen would've slaughtered him if they could see him now, yet they'd probably act the same way with someone like Grace pressed close.

"Moriah claims you give the best hugs, and I can't disagree,"

Grace murmured, "but I wanted to tell her that your kisses are even better."

Harrison lit up. It looked like he was getting his kiss. "You're the expert. Guess I can't argue with that."

She grinned and ran her hands up his chest, wrapping them around his neck. Harrison couldn't take it any longer, pulling her against him and pressing his lips to hers. The sweet nectar of her kiss was more delicious than anything he'd ever tasted.

Through the cloud of joy and endorphins, he heard his name being called repeatedly, until a banging on the door finally drew them apart. Harrison drew in quick pants of air, trying to clear his head.

"Harrison!" Jace's voice was more intense than he'd ever heard it. "Moriah put me in charge of keeping you moral. If I have to deadbolt Grace in her room, I will."

"As long as you deadbolt me in here with her." Harrison winked at her.

The door swung open, and Harrison was relieved that Jace didn't look mad at all. His blue eyes twinkled at them. "I checked your room first and Moriah gave me strict instructions to keep you two apart. 'No mac-daddying in my house!'" He mimicked her higher-pitched voice.

Harrison chuckled. "Don't worry. My intentions are honorable."

"I'm sure they are." Jace looked pointedly at Grace's mussed-up hair and red face. He pushed out a breath. "But I'm under strict instructions to get your backsides downstairs for treats and *Beauty and the Beast.*"

"You're going to make me sit through a movie when I could be kissing my girl? Who could possibly watch a movie at a time like this?" Harrison asked. He hoped he wasn't being too bold. Grace wasn't his girl, but he would do about anything at this point to make that phrase be true.

Grace was blushing prettily, like she had earlier today when Turk had called her his wife.

"I'm sure you'll get plenty of kissing in later." Jace pumped his eyebrows at Grace, then turned and led the way out into the hallway.

Harrison wrapped his arm around Grace and escorted her after Jace. He didn't mind spending the night cuddled with Grace watching a movie. He hoped he hadn't scared her away with his bold statements, but she'd been pretty forward, pulling him into her room and pushing him against the wall like that. He smiled at the remembrance. They could recreate that any time and he would be a happy man.

12

Moriah walked the two of them up to bed that night, their conscience and chaperone rolled into one. Grace didn't mind, as she absolutely adored Moriah. It was late enough that Grace didn't dare push her luck with her hostess and sneak into Harrison's room. She was shocked she'd been so bold with Harrison earlier, pulling him into her room and kissing him, but she didn't regret the time spent with him or the kiss. She lay down and drifted off to sleep, dreaming of that kiss and all things Harrison.

The next day, Turk had them up early and Moriah had a delicious breakfast casserole and cinnamon rolls waiting for them. They went to church together, and Grace should've been embarrassed at all the people she didn't know staring at her when she walked in with Harrison, but she was too happy being with him.

Harrison's parents came to church as well, and so did Moriah's close friends, Trin and Zander. Harrison's mama and Moriah both sang in the choir, and their beautiful voices brought emotion to Grace's heart she'd tried to ignore. She'd never blamed the good

Lord for taking her parents, but she'd felt such emptiness. Their praises to the Lord and adoration filled up the spots she thought would always be empty. She wouldn't be alone if she trusted in Him.

Harrison's leg brushed hers, and she glanced over at him. Had the Lord sent him to her? She wanted to never be alone again, but even more than that, she wanted it to be Harrison who filled that void. He reached for her hand and covered it with his, resting their clasped hands on his muscled thigh. Grace leaned against his shoulder and felt more than content just being close to him.

After church, they all went back to Harrison's parents' humble but well-kept split-level home for a barbecue. Harrison's mama was as round as his daddy was tall. His mama was just as friendly and open as Moriah. His daddy was much more reserved but very kind and welcoming. Moriah's friend, Trin, was a tall, gorgeous redhead, and her husband, Zander, was a lean, athletic-looking guy. They owned the bed and breakfast that Moriah used to work at, but also had a Southern mansion not far away from Moriah and Jace's. It seemed both the younger couples were ultra-wealthy.

They were about halfway through their barbecued chicken, coconut shrimp, corn on the cob, barbecued beans, and corn bread—delicious like only a Southern mama could make them—when Zander grinned at something his wife had said and Grace gasped out loud as recognition flooded her. "Oh my goodness, you were on *The Bachelor*, weren't you?" She hadn't missed an episode of that season, enamored with the handsome bachelor who'd seemed to have so much pain in his eyes.

Zander's smile froze. Trin was happy to answer for him. "Yes, and even with all those women chasing him, he came looking for me." She winked and squeezed his hand.

His grin came back again. "It was tough to run away from them all ... but worth it." He leaned over and kissed her.

"Good thing you're a fast runner," Trin said.

Moriah watched them with a broad grin on her face. "I had to do a little manipulating to make sure they didn't mess up the romance, but it all worked out in the end."

"I can't imagine you manipulating anyone, love," Jace said with a straight face.

She pushed at him. "Go on, you're the happiest man I know, no matter how I manipulate you—or rather, keep you in line."

Grace watched the couples tease each other, and then talk turned to Jace's twin brother, Nixon, who was expanding his Natural Nutrition Needs stores into the West Coast. Moriah wanted Nixon to get back home so she could set him up with a darling girl from their church.

"Not manipulative at all, my love." Jace winked.

Everyone laughed, Moriah loudest of all.

Feeling Harrison's gaze on her, Grace turned to him. He squeezed her hand and murmured, "Thanks for coming."

"Didn't have a lot of choice." It was fun to join in the teasing mood, but she quickly remedied her statement. "Thank you for bringing me. I needed this."

He nodded to her, looking like he wanted to say more, but Turk popped his head between them. "Uncle Hare, will you pass with me?"

"For sure." Harrison took his nephew's hand and left half his plate untouched. They walked a little ways off into the shady back-yard and caught and passed the ball. Harrison was ultra-gentle with his passes and cheered every time Turk caught them. He dove down low and jumped high or reached to the side, whatever he needed to do to make sure he caught the ball when Turk threw it.

"That boy of mine is pure gold."

Grace hadn't realized Harrison's mama had sat down next to

her, as caught up as she was in watching Harrison and Turk. "He is. You've done a fine job with both of your children, ma'am."

"Thank you, sweetheart. I'm mighty proud, that's for sure."

"As you should be."

His mama patted her hand, and they sat in silence while the rest of the table finished eating, still bantering back and forth and sharing funny stories about Jace's younger brother, Clay. Apparently, he was quite the overconfident crazy man.

Turk caught the ball and Harrison rushed for him, picked him up, and then tackled him softly to the grass. Turk shrieked with laughter, and Grace loved watching the interaction.

"My boy's never brought a girl home to meet me," his mama said in her low, melodious voice.

Grace tore her eyes from Harrison as he lifted Turk into the air, his biceps on fine display, and focused on his mama. "Is it okay that he brought me?"

"More than okay." His mama smiled. "I just want you to know that you must be very special and you're welcome here anytime."

"Thank you, ma'am."

"Oh, go on, it's Mama to you."

Grace had to bite at her lip not to cry. She missed her own mama every day. "Thank you, Mama."

Mama wrapped her up in a hug, and Grace savored the warmth and kindness of the embrace.

All too soon they were done eating, had cleaned up the food, and she and Harrison had to say their goodbyes. They'd left Uncle Mike and Aunt Geraldine long enough. Tomorrow they'd get back to work on Sycamore Bay, and hopefully the police would be able to find who was trying to burn it down. The heaviness of what they were heading back to pressed in on her, but the past day and a half had been the best reprieve she could've imagined. They hadn't done anything special, but just being around Harrison's family had been a dose of happy medicine.

"You come see me again soon, you hear?" Mama gave her another big squeeze.

"I will," Grace promised. She shook his daddy's hand and said goodbye to Trin and Zander, then walked out with Jace, Moriah, Turk, and Harrison.

Harrison held Turk in one arm and had the other wrapped around Grace. They stopped next to Harrison's Hyundai and Moriah gave them a stare down. "Now you two listen to me. I know how it is to want to kiss all night and then some."

"Hey, wait, don't you still want to do that?" Jace asked.

"Oh, hush, you." Moriah fixed him with a severe glare, but Jace smiled unrepentantly. She swung back to Harrison and Grace. "But the good Lord done gave us the wonderful blessing of finding each other, and if you're respecting his laws and waiting until marriage you'll be even more blessed, you hear me?"

"You know I'm going to respect Grace and the Lord," Harrison said in that deep baritone of his.

Grace was blushing again. Moriah was certainly direct. Marriage wasn't even on her radar. Harrison was amazing, but they'd known each other such a short time and she had a lot of other things to deal with before she settled down and married—namely her house and hopefully finishing her degree. "Yes, ma'am," she murmured.

"Oh, don't you ma'am me." Moriah reached out and gave her a hug. "You're going to be all alone in that house, and I know how temptation goes." She winked at Jace.

"I was too much temptation for her to ever resist," he said.

"Hush!" Moriah said, though she was laughing along with everyone else.

"Tempting me," Turk sang out.

"This conversation is probably too much for a four-year-old," Harrison said.

"Okay, give us hugs." Moriah hugged them both again. Jace gave Harrison a manly hug and a quick squeeze to Grace. Turk had the hardest time, clinging to his uncle's neck, then looking at Grace and saying, "I'm losing my beautifulest girlfriend."

"We'll see you again soon," Harrison promised.

Jace finally had to almost pry Turk off of Harrison. Then they were driving away and Grace already missed her new friends, who felt like family to her. The past two days hadn't just been a break from her reality; they'd been a huge change to her relationship with Harrison. He took her hand and hummed quietly along with the Christian radio as they drove. The time passed quickly as they reminisced about their childhoods, and before she knew it they were pulling up her oak-lined drive.

She sighed. It was good to be home, but a little overwhelming. She noticed more shingles missing on the roof, the lawn needed to be mowed again, the entire exterior needed repainting, and the porch railings sagged. She wasn't even close repainting the interior and paint was the least expensive material she needed. She couldn't fathom tackling the projects of replacing porch railings and the roof. How could her daddy let things get so run-down? The mansion was a mess and nothing close in size or details to Jace and Moriah's sprawling home, but it was hers and with time and money she could fix it all up. She frowned. She didn't have any money, and the house might not be hers much longer if she gave in to all the pressure to sell.

Uncle Mike and Aunt Geraldine gave them hugs but left pretty quick, though Uncle Mike found a moment to remind her that she was welcome to live with them anytime if she decided to sell and go back to school. Grace gave him the respect her parents would expect of her, but told him in no uncertain terms—No, thank you.

She was sick of the gentle reminders that selling would be best for her. She loved this house too much.

After they left, Uncle Mike acting more than a little put out with her and Aunt Geraldine soothing him as they walked away, Grace wasn't sure what to do with the evening. She was still full from all the lunch she'd consumed at Harrison's mama's, and they'd found a cooler full of food in the back of the car, next to their overnight bags. Moriah had sent leftover roast, potatoes, and veggies, as well as homemade bread, jam, cookies, and a stuffed pepper casserole. They wouldn't have to cook for a while.

Grace tried not to work on the house on Sundays so she couldn't keep busy painting or fixing up. If she'd been alone, she would've read a book, but she'd rather spend time with Harrison.

They unpacked the cooler, then took their bags to their rooms. She unloaded her clothes quickly. Pulling out her still-damp swimsuit, she had an idea. She walked down the hall to Harrison's room. The door was open and he was leaning over his suitcase. Dang, he was a fine-looking man.

He turned and saw her. "Hey." His slow smile spread.

She held the suit aloft. "Do you want to go swimming?"

"Sure. I was wondering if you ever swam in the bay, but then you never take any time off from working."

She laughed. "You got me there. Yeah, our bay is safe. Just the occasional alligator wanders over from the yonder swamp."

His eyes widened slightly. "So I might get the chance to fight an alligator for you?"

"You could only be so lucky." She batted her eyelashes at him.

"It's high on my list of lucky events."

"I'll just go change." She twirled the suit on her finger and turned toward the door. Harrison was by her side before she could exit the room. "Dang, you move fast."

He grinned and took her shoulders, backing her up into the

wall. "I just wanted to tell you that I really liked seeing you in your swimsuit last night."

"Well, then." She flushed from the compliment. "I'd think you'd want to let me go and put it on again."

"Later." His eyes swept over her face, lingering on her lips. He lowered his head and tenderly caressed her lips with his own. "Much later," he muttered huskily.

Grace dropped her swimsuit, wrapped her hands around his strong back, and didn't care if they ever went swimming.

13

It was much, much later when they made it to the bay. The sun was probably only half an hour from setting, but Harrison and Grace waded into the lukewarm water and he once again thoroughly enjoyed watching her swim in her one-piece suit.

The sun had set when they forced themselves out of the water and walked hand in hand up the long stretch of grass. "You work pretty hard for all those muscles?" Grace tilted her head to the side and studied him.

Harrison flexed his arm slightly. "Naw, I'm just built like this naturally."

Grace ran a hand over his shoulder. "How are you going to sit behind a desk all day? I can't imagine any of these muscles being dormant."

They reached the house. The night was warm, as usual, but they weren't being eaten alive by the mosquitoes yet. Harrison wrapped an arm around her thin waist and turned her to face him. The idea had been stewing for the past couple of days, but Moriah had pushed it to the forefront with her parting comments. Grace initiating the kiss last night and saying she couldn't imagine him behind a desk spurred his bravery to actually say something. This seemed like his moment.

"Grace, I enjoy numbers and I wouldn't hate being an accountant the rest of my life, but I have to tell you ... I love being here with you more. Much more."

She smiled. "I love having you here."

"I've been thinking about your problem—you know, with the house—and I just came up with the perfect solution." He wanted to tell her that he loved her, but she might not believe him. They'd only known each other a week and he didn't want it to seem insincere when he confessed how he'd fallen for her, but this needed to be said now. They needed to act so she didn't lose her house, and they needed to stay together so he could protect her and find whoever was trying to either scare her into selling or burn her house down.

"I think we should get married." The words came out in a rush, and he felt immense relief. He'd done it. She'd know this was the solution and soon he'd get brave enough to confess his love for her as well.

Grace took a step back from him, her brow wrinkled, her eyes cloudy. "You didn't just say that."

Harrison hurried to explain. "It's the perfect solution. You'll get what you need for Sycamore Bay and I'll be here to take care of you, to protect you, and you can adopt as many children as you want and I'll help you." He stopped, not sure why she was shaking her head at his reasoning. He hadn't even gotten into how he wouldn't be stuck behind a desk and she could finish her schooling and he could someday pursue his own dreams of coaching football.

She studied him with tight lips, then finally said, "No."

"No?" That single syllable was a sledgehammer to the gut. She didn't want him.

Grace stared at him for a few seconds, then whirled and banged through the back door and into the house. Harrison stood there. She'd turned him down. He wasn't sure how long he stood there, feeling weak and dejected and wondering how he would ever get over Grace. Apparently his brilliant idea wasn't so brilliant. He probably should've slowed down and thought it out, expressed it a little better, or had some patience. Gotten to know her for longer than a week, maybe?

He pushed out a long breath, then let himself in the back door, wearily climbed the stairs, and gathered his stuff. He assumed Grace was in her room, but he didn't go check. What did he have left to say? She had plenty she could say. She could stop him. She could explain why she said no. She could say yes, she'd marry him. But the house was quiet and chilly—for the first time since he'd been here—as he packed, still wearing his damp swimsuit. He could shower when he got back to Montgomery.

He'd spent most of his life being admired for his looks or his athletic prowess. He'd assumed Grace had seen past all of that to the real him, cared about how he treated her, how great they got along, his willingness to work hard, and talk through things with her. He'd been wrong. Apparently, he'd never be more than the stud who could look good and run fast. He grunted in disgust, not liking his pity party but unable to stop it.

He carried his suitcase past her room without stopping, down the stairs, and exited through the back door where he could lock it. Each step hurt, not physically but deep down inside. He hated to leave her, but she didn't want him, didn't need him. He couldn't stay here with her "no" ringing in his head. The outside nighttime air was warm, stale, and reeked of hopelessness.

He climbed into his SUV, grateful to push the start button and blast the air conditioning, though the noise was too loud and abrasive right now. Harrison dialed the police detective they'd worked with and explained quickly that he had to leave, and could he please send someone by to be here with Grace tonight? The detective promised they'd be there within half an hour. Harrison would hire a private security company himself in the morning. No matter how viciously Grace had ripped him apart, he didn't want anything happening to her. The detective agreeing to his request helped him feel marginally better.

He pulled quickly out of the driveway. The dark road slid by underneath his car. He'd drive back to Montgomery and tell his boss he'd failed. The prospect of gaining Henry's clients was gone, and he might even lose his job. Jace, Nixon, and Zander had all offered to hire him out of college. He'd wanted to make his way on his own, but that was silly. He could work for one of them and be happy. Well, happy was stretching it without Grace. He could be busy.

14

Grace lay curled into a ball and listened like a hawk. Listened to Harrison pack up his bag, listened to him walk past her room without stopping, listened to the finality of the back door closing. All she could hear was his deep, wonderful voice asking her, "No?"

Why couldn't she have screamed, "Yes! Of course I'll marry you, you amazing, wonderful, kind man!"

But that was so unfair to him. He didn't really know her, couldn't possibly love her. He'd said nothing about love. He truly was an accountant: it was all about crunching the numbers, and him offering to marry her had seemed so analytical and thought-out. It was also thoughtful and kind, and she refused to be a charity case, especially to this perfect and handsome and superb man who she still thought of as the football hero, even though he was so much more to her than that now.

His car engine fired. She rolled onto her stomach and screamed into her pillow. Could it be possible that he'd just offered for the money? They would both be worth a whole lot of money with her inheritance. She didn't think Harrison was the type of man to want a marriage of convenience just so he'd be wealthy. He'd sounded so altruistic, like he was doing it for her, for the children, but he'd originally come here for money so who knew?

He'd kissed her like the sun wouldn't shine tomorrow. He'd called her "his girl." Obviously he cared for her. Was it enough?

His car lights pulled away and the fear of losing him raced through her. She scrambled off her bed and sprinted for the back staircase. Maybe he didn't love her yet, but he did care for her. She'd told him no without even talking about it. It was possible he loved her and that his intentions to marry her were sincere and pure like she'd come to expect with Harrison.

She pumped down the stairs and was out the back door in seconds. "Harrison!" she screamed. "Stop! Please stop!"

A hand covered her mouth and she was knocked to the spongy grass next to the back porch. Disoriented, she peered past the pain in her head and into Beau's blue eyes.

"Beau?" she muttered.

"I'm here," he said, which seemed like a weird comment. How could he know Harrison had left her and her life was a mess? Or was he here to try to hurt her and her house?

The ground rumbled underneath her as if an earthquake was happening. A whoosh of light caught her eye and she looked up. A huge fireball exploded out of the top floor of her home, spraying shingles, plaster, and bits of wood into the air. Grace screamed, pushed away from Beau, and jumped to her feet. Her body shook uncontrollably as she cried out in horror. Sycamore Bay. Her house. Another loud blast rocked the earth and the house exploded outward—windows shattering and wood flung everywhere. She was thrown onto her back. Her head slammed onto the concrete patio. Her last conscious thought was wondering if Harrison would ever know that she loved him.

15

Harrison heard a loud boom. He slammed on his brakes and whirled, seeing the fireball above the tree line.

"Grace!" Her name ripped from his throat. Spinning his car around, he jammed the gas pedal to the floor and prayed like he'd never prayed in his life. "Please, Lord, protect her. Please!" he begged over and over again.

He pushed the button on his steering wheel, and when Siri asked him to please say a command, he said, "Call 911." Another boom rattled through his chest and fear took his breath away.

Seconds later the call connected and he yelled, "There's been an explosion." He was amazed he could remember the address. He begged for fire trucks and medical help, then hung up on the operator.

As he flew up the driveway, horror clawed at his gut. Grace's house was an inferno, fire and smoke pouring from the roof, the windows, the doors. And he'd left her in there. How could he have left? He should be there with her.

What could he do in there? Die with her? Yes! Grace was in there. He gasped for air and tears streaked down his face. He jammed the vehicle into park and jumped out, trying to see a point of entry, some way to get to her.

"Grace! Grace!" he screamed over and over again. The tall front doors spouted fire and smoke. He covered his head with his arm and tried to get up the steps, but the heat pushed him back.

No, no, no! Not Grace. Please, Lord, Please!

He ran around to the back of the house, hoping, praying for some way to get in and get to her. His brain tried to tell him that she was gone, that there was no hope, but his heart would not accept it.

"Grace!" he hollered. "Please, Grace!"

A man rose into his field of vision. "Help me," he croaked.

As Harrison sprinted toward him, the flames outlined the good-looking face and blond hair. Beau. Harrison reared back. "Grace?" he managed.

"She's here. Help me lift her away."

Harrison caught his first full breath. Grace had made it out?

He ran to the spot Beau indicated, and it was true. Grace was lying on her side in the grass. He didn't think of any rules of correct emergency techniques as he rolled her over and lifted her into his arms. He felt the sweetest exhalation of breath and murmured, "Oh, thank you, Lord." Then he ran toward the water. If the fire got even more out of control, the water had to be the safest place.

When he reached the edge of the bay, he knelt there on the beach and tried to think how to check her more thoroughly. She was breathing, but what else could be wrong?

Beau knelt next to them. "Is she okay?"

"You stay away from her!" he roared. Grace was alive and he

would forever praise the Lord for that, but this guy had started the fire and had no right to ask if she was okay.

"Hey, man. I came to save her."

"You did this!" Harrison jerked his head toward Grace's beloved house, burning out of control.

"I wouldn't do this. I love her!" He pointed to the edge of the woods. "They did this." Two men's shadows stood, silently watching the fire take Grace's home, her every memory of her parents and her innocent, happy childhood.

Harrison's eyes widened, then narrowed. "Stay with her," he murmured, setting Grace gently on the sand. He stood and sprinted for the trees. The men noticed him and started running. Harrison put on speed and tackled the taller of the two.

Sirens blared through the night. The other man was escaping, but Harrison figured if he caught one, hopefully his prisoner or Beau would rat out the other one. The whole thing was making him dizzy. Had he really just left Grace in that snake Beau's care to chase after her arsonist?

The man struggled in his arms, but Harrison was an expert at wrapping a body up. He put a stranglehold on the guy and then jerked him to his feet, dragging him back to Beau and Grace and hopefully the cops who would be there soon. As they got closer to the fire, the man fighting and writhing against him came into view with the help of the flames.

Harrison almost lost his grip. "Uncle Mike!"

Mike glared at him.

"How could you?" Harrison asked.

"How could I?" Mike snarled at him. "How could *they*?" He gestured to the house. "The entire Addison family owed me every-thing. I'm the one who kept this place running all my life. Addison always wanted to help everybody, and he would've given his entire fortune away if it wasn't for me. They owed me everything, but Addison would never listen to my visions and thought he was doing me some favor leaving me enough money for a pitiful cottage." He was frothing with anger now. "If Grace would've sold to Steele, I would've gotten my piece of the brilliant resort I've always planned to build here. But she wouldn't sell, so I finally had to kill her. I was next in line on the will and now I'll have everything."

They were almost to Beau and Grace now. Grace still wasn't moving, and all Harrison wanted to do was wake her up and hold her.

"You didn't kill her." Harrison jerked the man around so he could see Grace's beautiful face. "Take him to the police," Harrison commanded Beau. "And tell them where your father went. He was the other man, correct?"

Beau nodded, looking meek for possibly the first time in his life. He stood and grabbed Mike's arm in a death grip. "I stole their boat keys so they couldn't escape," he told Harrison.

Harrison finally understood why Mike and Beau's dad were still close by, but Beau's help was too little, too late in his mind.

"You idiot, Beau!" Mike yelled, straining to free himself. "Use that little brain for a second! You lose everything if I get arrested."

"No. I take over my father's legit businesses while you two rot in prison for what you tried to do to Gracie Lee." Beau seemed to have strength beyond his own as he jerked the older man toward the front of the house, where police cars, emergency vehicles, and fire trucks crowded the driveway.

"Send the paramedics back here," Harrison said.

Beau nodded.

Harrison knelt next to Grace again, starting his prayers up more diligently. He gently touched her head and neck, finding some bumps on the back of her head, and started to despair that she wouldn't wake up. Firefighters ran toward them, and Harrison wanted them to hurry and help her, wake her up so he could tell her how sorry he was. How could he have ever left her?

They put a neck brace on and carefully lifted her on a stretcher. Harrison followed behind them as they hurried back to the ambulance. All the while, she didn't wake up. When they reached the ambulance and loaded her in, Harrison tried to climb up with them.

"Are you her husband?" A large firefighter blocked his entrance.

"No, but ..."

"Sorry. Family only."

"Harrison?" Her voice floated out to him.

Harrison shoved the guy out of the way and scrambled into the narrow spot next to the stretcher. Grace's beautiful blue eyes were open. They weren't clear or particularly lucid, but they were open.

"You're here?" Her gaze swept over him, full of hope for a better tomorrow.

"I'm never leaving you again," he whispered fiercely.

She smiled slightly. "I love you." Then she closed her eyes again.

"You need to get out." The guy he'd pushed out of the way looked like he was ready to wrestle Harrison out of the ambulance.

Harrison looked to the other firefighter for help. He was smaller than the first, but with the word "Captain" on his helmet. He looked between Harrison and Grace, then said firmly, "You can ride with us."

"Thank you, sir." Harrison settled into a seat as the doors were slammed. While one firefighter took Grace's stats, the other sat at the head of the stretcher, and even though she had the neck brace on, he held her head steady like he was keeping her from being flung around. The vehicle started moving. Grace might be unconscious again, but she had to know. Harrison bent down close and said, "I love you too."

She didn't open her eyes, but she did smile.

16

E very part of Grace hurt, but her head took the prize. She tried to open her eyes, but it was too bright out there. Someone was holding her hand, and then she smelled that clean, manly scent. She couldn't open her eyes, but she did find the strength to squeeze his hand.

She could feel Harrison lean closer and whisper huskily, "Grace?"

"Can't ... open ... my ... eyes," she ground out.

"You'll be okay. The doc says every part of you is okay, but your lips might need a little TLC from yours truly."

She smiled, but that hurt too, her lips felt cracked and swollen. "If you ... find me some chapstick and a breath mint," she muttered.

He laughed. "Consider it done." He brushed his free hand gently over her forehead. Grace couldn't stand it any longer; she forced her eyes open, and his handsome face and wide smile beamed back at her. She drank in the sight of him before closing her eyes again.

"It's okay, my love. Go back to sleep. Sleep as long as you need. I'll be here."

Grace squeezed his hand tighter. She wanted to sleep, but she needed to know. "Do you really ..." She swallowed hard and licked her lips. "Love me?"

Harrison's low chuckle washed over her. "Oh, Grace." He softly brushed her lips with his. "I love you more than Jace loves Moriah."

She smiled at that and drifted back into the darkness.

When she awoke again, her lips tasted like her vanilla mint lip gloss. It didn't hurt quite as bad to open her eyes this time and she blinked, searching until she found Harrison slumped in a chair next to her bed. He looked exhausted and beat up, but absolutely irresistible to her. She stared at him as long as she could stand to have her eyes open, then let them drift shut and shifted on the bed to relieve the ache in her lower back.

She must've made too much noise, because Harrison's eyes popped open and he leaned closer to her. "Grace? Love? You need anything?"

She shook her head slowly, licking her lips. "This is my favorite lip gloss. Where did you find it?"

"Would you believe you left your purse in the back seat of my car?"

"I did?" She remembered putting her purse there when they left Moriah's, but she'd forgotten it when they unloaded their overnight bags at home. The thought made all of her other losses not quite as horrible. Her house was gone, but she still had her purse.

Her house was gone. Sycamore Bay was nothing but ashes. Despair crashed over her and tears spilled down her cheeks. "Is it a total loss?" she whispered.

Harrison pushed a hand through his short hair. "I'm sorry."

She swallowed hard and let the tears fall. All the memories with her parents, Uncle Mike, and Aunt Geraldine. The history of generations of her family who built, loved, and lived in that house. Pictures and family heirlooms ... but most of all, she remembered the love that permeated the walls themselves.

Harrison took her hand but didn't say anything. He let her cry. The tears washed some of the pain and sleepiness from her eyes, but made the rest of her ache for what was lost. Finally, she couldn't stand to sit and cry much longer. She pushed the button to raise her bed up higher. She knew more tears would come—the pain of losing her home wouldn't go away anytime soon—but at least Harrison was here.

Harrison straightened. "Can I get you anything?"

"Besides my favorite lip gloss?" She smiled at him. "The breath mint."

Harrison laughed and pulled a packet of Breath Savers from his pocket, placing a couple into her hand.

"Thank you." Grace savored the peppermint flavor.

"Oh, Grace. I'd do anything for you."

She knew it was true, and even though her eyes should've run out of water, a few more tears leaked out. She wiped them away. "Thank you."

"So ..." He pumped his eyebrows. "What is your wish, my love?"

"Ice water would be brilliant."

"That was easy." He grabbed a cup filled with water and lifted it close to her.

She wrapped her lips around the plastic straw and sucked down the icy goodness tinged with peppermint. When she'd had enough, she leaned back. "Thank you. So the doctors say I'm okay?"

"Yes. You had a pretty good concussion, but no broken bones. As soon as you feel up to it, they said they'll release you."

"It was Beau." She didn't want to admit it, but she had to. Her old friend was truly a horrific person. "He blew it up so his dad could develop the property."

"No." Harrison studied her for a few agonizing seconds before admitting, "His dad and ... Mike did."

"Mike? Uncle Mike?"

He nodded. "Set it all up while we were gone and Aunt Geraldine was sleeping."

"Oh no." Tears rushed to the surface and she wished she'd never cry again in her life. "Why? How could he?" She sniffled and wiped at her nose.

Harrison stood and leaned over, gently hugging her. Grace clung to his arms and his tenderness about undid her. After a few minutes, he sat down and reached for her hand. "I think he twisted it all in his mind. He felt like you and your dad owed the place to him because of all the work he did and his ancestors always working there."

"I never even knew he felt that way." Her heart was so heavy. First her Sycamore Bay and now Uncle Mike? "Aunt Geraldine too?"

"No." Harrison shook his head firmly. "She knew nothing about it. Mike even affirmed that. She's so distraught. It's sad to watch how sick she is about it all. She's been here checking on you."

Grace felt marginally better. At least she hadn't been betrayed by Aunt Geraldine too. Then it hit her all over again, like a wrecking ball that kept swinging back and forth and doing almost as much damage with each swing. Her home was gone. Homeless was a horrific word. What did she do now? "Where am I going to live?"

Harrison's eyes got that smoldering look she loved. "I've been thinking about that while you've slept and slept."

She laughed.

"Like Sleeping Beauty." He pressed his lips to her forehead.

"Ha!" She certainly didn't feel like a beauty right now.

"You're more beautiful than ever," Harrison murmured. "And I've been thinking if I asked you to marry me, and if I did a little better job of it than last time—" He winked. "—then we can be together and rebuild your house and make and adopt babies until we're insanely busy and insanely happy."

Grace stared at him.

The pause dragged on until Harrison cleared his throat and his smile became nervous. "What do you think?"

"I have two conditions," she said.

He exhaled and smiled. "Name them."

"Number one: I want more bathrooms when we remodel, even if we have to lose a bedroom upstairs to do it."

"Okay. That's an easy one."

"Number two ..." She grinned. "I want a real proposal one of these times, with a ring and a kiss and flowery words."

Harrison chuckled. "I'll plan the best proposal you've ever seen, but ... can I have a kiss right now?"

"Yes, sir."

He leaned close. Grace breathed in his manly scent and forgot about every ache and pain as he kissed her. The promise and joy in their future stretched before her, stopping the wrecking ball and the fear of being alone ever again.

EPILOGUE

Grace lifted the ponytail off her neck to fan herself and gave the tire swing another heave. Ivy and Lily giggled and clung to each other in the swing. "Higher, Mama, higher," Ivy begged.

Grace and Harrison had officially adopted the three-year-old twin girls on their one-year wedding anniversary in July. Grace arched her back to stop the ache from the twin boys kicking each other inside her abdomen. She'd hoped to fill their home with children, and they had a good start already.

Harrison came out of the house carrying a tray of sandwiches, chips, and veggies; Aunt Geraldine followed him with iced lemonade and cups. Harrison caught Grace's eye and grinned. Her stomach swooped. Would she ever stop being so enamored with her handsome husband? She hoped not.

She was so proud of him for all he'd accomplished the past two years. They had used the house insurance to rebuild Sycamore Bay and carefully invested the money from her daddy, but set aside enough to fund a sports program for underprivileged youth, organizing competitive teams for those who showed talent, dedication, and wanted to play at the next level. Harrison paid for the coaches, team fees, and travel for the players. Of course he coached the football team, but he also had volleyball, soccer, and lacrosse and was working on adding basketball and baseball. He was the most amazing coach with his brilliance with numbers and ability to read the field.

Grace loved watching him get right in there with the teenagers and push them physically to the next level. Their teams had proven to be successful and he had more than one triumphant story of bringing young people off the streets or saving them from drugs or crime. Next year, several of his players would be playing at the collegiate level thanks to his contacts and the opportunities he'd given them.

"Come on, girls," Aunt Geraldine called. "You eat all this yummy lunch, and then I'm going to read you a story before your surprise comes."

Grace held on to the chain of the swing and pulled it to a stop. The girls scrambled off. Ivy fell to the grass, but hopped up and hurried to the patio table. The child never cried, no matter what happened to her. Sometimes it worried Grace when she thought about the abuse her beautiful brunette girls endured their first year and a half of life, but they were both happy and well-adjusted now.

Harrison set his load down and stopped for a kiss from each of his girls before he reached her side. "Hi, beautiful. You keeping cool enough?"

"You worry about me too much. I'm only ten and half months pregnant."

Harrison chuckled low and deep. "These little boys proving too much for you, Mrs. Jackson?"

"I'm a tough Southern woman. No man could get the best of me." She winked.

"Well, you've got their daddy wrapped tight around your pinky finger, so I'm sure the boys will follow suit when they finally arrive." He touched her abdomen with reverence, then kissed her. "I love you."

"I love you more."

Ivy and Lily giggled behind them.

"Stop mooning over each other and come eat," Aunt Geraldine called.

A car motored up the driveway, but they couldn't see it from back here. They'd built the house almost entirely like the original, except for more bathrooms upstairs like Grace had wanted, and it was amazing to have everything new and low-maintenance, especially the air conditioning unit. They'd also put in a swimming pool and a large outdoor patio and pool house and fixed up the yard with all the flowers Grace had dreamed of. A gazebo graced the huge oak tree with the tire swing in it.

"Who is it?" Lily cried out. She scrambled off her chair and around the house.

"Oh heavens, they'll never eat now," Aunt Geraldine said, but her eyes twinkled.

Turk came racing around the side of the house, about knocking his younger cousin off her feet. "Lily!" He picked her up and swung her around, showing off his six-year-old strength. Lily's peals of laughter lit the air, and Ivy hurried to reach her cousin as well.

Jace escorted Moriah much more slowly around the house. Moriah's abdomen was almost as badly distended as Grace's.

Harrison wrapped his arm around Grace and they went to meet the other couple, enjoying watching Turk and his cousins hug and laugh together.

"How are you feeling, sis?" Moriah greeted Grace.

"Huge. You?"

"Massive." Moriah wrapped her hands underneath her stomach. "What do you say we have these babies today?"

"If you've got a formula to induce labor, I'd be all over it."

Moriah laughed long and low. "You've still got five weeks left. I'm the one who should be any day."

"I'm bigger than you."

"No." Moriah shook her head, though it was probably true.

Jace gave Grace a side hug. "You two are both beautiful."

"Thank you, my schmoozer of a husband," Moriah said.

Harrison nodded. "The two of us are the luckiest men I know."

"Ah, and you're rubbing off on my strong, silent type of husband," Grace told Jace.

"What?" Harrison turned to her. "I tell you you're beautiful all the time."

"I know, love, but you're still strong and—when you kiss me—silent."

"I guess I'd better get kissing you, then." He bent down and kissed her, and she forgot about being far too pregnant and the crowd they had watching them. With Harrison close, everything was just about perfect.

ABOUT THE AUTHOR

Cami is a part-time author, part-time exercise consultant, part-time housekeeper, full-time wife, and overtime mother of four adorable boys. Sleep and relaxation are fond memories. She's never been happier.

Sign up for Cami's newsletter to receive a free ebook copy of *The Resilient One: A Billionaire Bride Pact Romance* and information about new releases, discounts, and promotions here.

If you enjoyed Harrison and Grace's story, I think you would love Jace and Moriah's story. Read on for a sneak peek of *Cancun Getaway: A Billionaire Beach Romance*.

www.camichecketts.com
cami@camichecketts.com

EXCERPT FROM CANCUN GETAWAY

Moriah tilted her head back and let the sun kiss her face. They'd landed in Cancun two hours ago, and a driver had brought them and their friends Trin and Zander straight to the upscale, all-inclusive resort. She and her three-year old, Turk, had changed into their suits first thing and headed straight for the beach. They were having the time of their lives digging in the sand.

The resort was massive. The buildings housing the rooms had eight or nine floors, depending on if they boasted a penthouse or not. The resort was shaped like a horseshoe with the open end to the beach. All of the pools, restaurants, and spa area were in the center. The beach was just a flight of stairs below the pools, separated by a retaining wall, waterfalls, and infinity pools, with most of the pools and rooms overlooking the glorious ocean. Yay for paradise.

"Shovel, Mama!" Turk commanded.

"Demanding, demanding." Moriah knelt on the sand and put a hand on her hip, tossing her black curls. "You don't boss *the* Mama around."

Turk giggled. "*Please* shovel, Mama. I need tracks for my monster truck."

She smiled and dug in. His track was already extensive, but she'd do anything for her little man. As Turk pushed the truck around the track making zoom noises, Moriah savored the sound of the waves. Living in Montgomery, Alabama her entire life, she'd made it to Gulf Shores a few times. It wasn't like this was her first time at the ocean, but it was definitely her first time on white-sand-Caribbean beaches, and she was in heaven.

Trin and Zander hadn't made it down from their room yet. *Dang newly-married lovers,* she thought, but she was happy for them. She couldn't believe they'd talked her into leaving the bed and breakfast for over a week. Trin and Zander owned the Cloverdale. The mansion had been in Trin's family for generations, and Moriah felt like the restored bed and breakfast was her home too, and Trin was closer to her than family. In fact, they liked to claim they were sisters just to see people's reactions. Moriah smiled thinking about people's reactions. Trin was a tall, beautiful redhead, and Moriah was petite and as brown as her mama's mahogany bookcases.

A group of young adults were playing volleyball about fifty yards down the beach, and Moriah found her gaze drawn in that direction. Three of the men looked like they could be triplets from this distance—tall, blond, and too good-looking for their own good. Her brother Harrison was always teasing her that she had vanilla fever, but he knew better than anybody that blond men just spelled heartache and trouble for her. Why was it they could steal her eyeballs from their intended target? A pair of nice blue eyes could give her heart palpitations. It didn't help that she never had time to date and hardly met any single men her age working in a bed and breakfast that catered to couples. Luckily, she always stayed strong where blond men were concerned, or at least, she had for the past three years.

One of the men glanced her way for a third time and gave her a broad smile. His teal-blue eyes were beckoning to her as his tanned cheek crinkled with an irresistible grin. Moriah returned the smile, but quickly refocused on digging the track. Sheesh, she thought she was used to heat and humidity, but she was suddenly burning up. *Lord, give me strength to resist the white hottie.* She chuckled to herself. As if the man was going to chase her around the resort. There were plenty of women taking part in the volleyball game who looked more than happy to hang on his every muscle.

"Mama, look." Turk pointed out at the gently rolling waves where some teenage girls were trying to stand up on paddle-boards. They squealed as a larger wave came along and knocked both of them into the water.

"Let's do that," Turk said.

Moriah sprang up. She was more than ready to try anything and everything in this tropical paradise. Volleyball topped the list, even though she wasn't any good at the actual sport. She chanced another glance at her blond Adonis. Just her luck that he was serving the ball at that moment. His muscles rippled underneath his tanned skin. A moment later, the other team returned his serve. He dove to save the ball, and she had to look away or risk diving after him herself.

He stood, brushing sand from his shredded abdomen and then caught her eye again. Oh. My. Goodness. Hopefully, paddle boarding would cool her off. A tall redhead bee-bopped up to Moriah's Adonis and placed her hands on his chest, drawing his attention away from Moriah. Of course he had women draping themselves all over him. Look at the guy.

Turk was already skipping down the beach in the opposite

direction of the volleyball net. Moriah hurried after him and found the resort worker who provided beach equipment. Within minutes, they had lifejackets, instructions, a paddle, and a long board in the water that was, unfortunately, not one bit stable.

Moriah placed Turk on the board then knelt behind him, grasping the paddle. They were only inches deep, and one wave shot them back onto the beach.

"Come on, Mama. Let's go." Turk demanded.

"I'm trying, little man." Moriah pushed off the sand hard with the paddle, and they moved a few feet. She started paddling ferociously but had to lift the paddle to the other side of the board and over Turk's head every few strokes. They'd turn one direction then the other and were making very little progress as waves kept pushing them in. She needed to stand up to paddle more effectively and make any headway against the gentle waves.

"Okay, buddy. Hold on." They were only in a foot of water so it wouldn't matter if they tipped, but it felt awkward, as if the people in lounge chairs on the beach were watching them. What about her volleyball-playing Adonis? She hoped he wasn't anywhere nearby.

Slowly, she stood, flexing her abs to help her balance. Her legs trembled, and she couldn't even think about paddling. She simply tried to stay upright. A wave rolled toward them. As it lifted one side of the board, Moriah let out a yelp, but she rode through it and miraculously didn't fall in. Turk was cheering. "Yeah!"

"Whew. That was a close one."

"Good job, Mama. Now, can you *please* paddle faster? I wanna surf!"

"I'll try." She doubted they'd do anything close to surfing, but she had to try for her boy. Shakily, she inserted the paddle into the water and pushed off the sand. Her legs wobbled. They moved a few inches. Moriah lifted the paddle to the other side. The board bobbed and, before she could do much more than cry out, flipped them both off.

Moriah was able to stay on her feet and only landed in a foot of water. Turk got dunked, but his life jacket kept him floating. She hurriedly grabbed him and lifted him out. "Are you okay?"

Turk grinned. "We're bad at this, Mama."

She laughed. "Yes, my man, we are."

"Would you like a little help?" a deep voice asked from behind her. Moriah whirled around, and her eyes widened. Adonis had been good from afar, but he was miles past good up close. She brushed the curls from her face and swallowed hard.

"We're just newbies, but we're scrappy. We'll figure it out." She arched an eyebrow and gave him a saucy swirl of her hips. It wasn't a conscious flirtation, just natural instinct. Trin always teased her that she danced her way through life.

He grinned, set his paddle on his board, and pushed it back onto the beach. How had he gotten a board without her even noticing? He had a lifejacket on so at least his chest and abdomen was covered, but his shoulders and arms were picture-perfect enough to make her need one of those specialty drinks the waiters kept offering. "Wouldn't it be more fun to try it together?"

"If you're sure you're up for a lesson." Did he have a slight Southern accent? His voice reminded her of somebody who'd grown up in the South then had it knocked out of them by Northern schooling and a rich lifestyle.

"No issue sharing my expertise with a beautiful woman."

"I meant me teaching you." She pointed her finger at him, grinning at her sauciness. Of course, she couldn't teach him anything but dance moves.

"Oh?" He chuckled easily. "I like the sound of that." Wading into the water, he held out his arms to her boy. "Do you want to ride with me, buddy? Then your sister will have an easier time teaching us how it's done."

Moriah opened her mouth to correct his assumption. She wasn't surprised as she was mistaken for Turk's sister and aunt a lot. Unfortunately, Turk interrupted her. "Sure!" He hollered.

Moriah loved how Turk's "sure" always came out as a happy "shore." As he launched himself into the man's arms, Moriah scrambled for her boy, but came up empty. Turk was naturally friendly with everyone, but he especially loved large men who tossed him in the air.

Moriah stared at the two of them together, and the world around her seemed to settle. The tall, good-looking, tanned man holding her little boy with his smooth, brown skin and curly hair made quite the picture. She wished she was a painter and could capture this moment. The contrast of the man and her child, yet the absolute rightness of them both, combined with the beach and the ocean was simply beautiful.

Adonis pulled his board out and settled Turk on it, handing him the large paddle. "How old are you, buddy?"

"Me three!" Turk called out happily.

"I think that's big enough to steer for a minute while I help the beautiful lady. Then I'll come take you into the deep water."

"Okay. Sure."

The way Turk said "shore" was so stinking cute it brought a quick smile to Adonis' face. Moriah had to clench her hands to keep from reaching out and touching that bronzed cheek. Adonis turned to her, and her breath caught in her throat.

"Okay. Let me help you up."

"I told you I've got it," Moriah said quickly, scrambling onto the board with the paddle in hand. It tipped one way and then the other, and before she could react, she was in the water again.

Adonis caught her around the waist. Moriah looked up, and those blue eyes twinkled at her. "Oh, Lord have mercy." She muttered.

His grin widened as he plucked her up out of the water like she was a sack of sugar and planted her on the board. It wobbled, but he kept her steady. Moriah glanced over at Turk who was happily splashing with his paddle just a few feet away. Adonis' hands were at her waist as he reached up to help her. He kept his gaze on her face as he moved his hands to just above her knees. Moriah gasped. If there was a more sensual move or way a man could look at a woman, she sure hadn't seen or experienced it.

It was definitely time for some sass. She was in danger of falling for the tall hottie before she even learned his name and possibly throwing herself into a bigger mess than the last one she'd been in with a blue-eyed blond. She was older now and much more mature and sensible, so she couldn't fall into that trap again, right?

"I think you can take your hands off, thank you very much," she said as tartly as she could.

His eyebrows lifted. "You sure you ready to fly solo?"

"Been doing it my whole life."

"Really? Why?"

He still hadn't removed his stinking hands from her legs, and she was quivering with the wonderful sensation of it all. Thankfully, Turk was oblivious, happily patting the water and singing to himself.

"When you reach mama status at seventeen, you grow up fast." She pinned him with a look. There, that should stop his flirting. She was a mama, and no matter how challenging the path to sunshine had been, she was proud of Turk and thrilled with every moment of her life now. She was also very leery where good-looking blond men were concerned.

"You're a mother?" Finally, his hands dropped. Fortunately, she didn't plummet into the water, but stayed swaying on the board.

He looked over at Turk then back at her. His jaw low. "No, really? I thought maybe a nephew or brother."

She fell off the stinking board again, splashing into the water next to him. "Nope, he's my boy. Come on, Turk. Let's go."

"No, Mama, we didn't have a ride."

"We can't crush a little boy's dreams." Adonis winked at her then waded through the water to where Turk perched on his board. The man pushed away from the shore, easily stepped up behind Turk, and started paddling away.

"W-wait." Moriah had frozen when he left her in the shallow water. She quickly regained her senses, knelt on her board, and paddled to try to keep up. Again, she went one direction then another, but she couldn't get anywhere close to him.

Turk laughed gleefully as they zoomed over waves and out past the buoys.

"Slow down!" She screamed at the man's broad, retreating shoulders. She knew he wasn't really going to steal her child, but it just felt wrong that she wasn't right next to Turk.

Adonis glanced over his shoulder and smirked at her. "You're looking great."

The nerve, the absolute nerve of the man.

"Come on, Mama." Turk called happily. "Whee! I'm surfing." He put his chubby arms out and laughed so cutely.

"You're not supposed to go past the buoys." She hollered at Adonis' back.

The man turned a smooth circle and stroked easily back toward her. His board bumped into hers, and Turk laughed. Moriah stayed on her knees, relief whooshing through her. She didn't like her son to be too far away.

"Sorry. I didn't hear that rule," he said, looking unrepentant as he grinned at her.

Moriah was mad, which was completely unlike her. She always rolled with life and kept a smile on her face, but right now, this guy ticked her off. Taking off with her boy like that was completely out of line. "Don't you dare try to steal my boy or I'll hogtie you and beat you with a stick."

"Where are you from?" he asked. Rather than scare him, her threats seemed to create more interest in his eyes.

"Excuse me?" What did that have to do with the price of bacon?

"You talk like home."

Before he'd taken off with her child, back when he had those strong hands on her waist and then her legs, she'd felt a sense of home from him too.

"Montgomery, Alabama." She lifted her chin. Proud as proud could be of her Southern upbringing.

"I'm from Mountain Green."

"Figures." She spat. "All the rich hotties live there." Mountain Green was an ultra-wealthy suburb of Birmingham, about an hour and a half north of her home.

He lifted an eyebrow.

"Let's surf, Mister." Turk pounded on the surfboard with his open palms.

"Do you care if we go on another ride if we stay within the buoys?"

"Thank you for having the courtesy to ask this time."

He grinned. "Sometimes us rich hotties remember our social graces."

A laugh erupted from her before she could contain it. The man stared at her. It was one of those intense, sensual looks she'd only seen in the movies and sometimes when she caught Zander staring at her friend, Trin. It dried up her laughter quickly, and she wondered if she needed to jump off her board and into the ocean.

"Do that again." He murmured.

"What?" She pushed at her curly locks.

"Laugh."

"Why?"

"That was the most beautiful sound I've ever heard."

A charmer too, Moriah thought as warmth darted through her. Just like that, he'd taken away her frustrations, but at the same time terrified her. Turk's daddy, Brock, had also been a charmer.

"Paddle, please," Turk said.

"Sure!" The man winked at her. "I'm coming back for more of that laughter though." With that, he paddled away. Turk's giggles floated back to her.

Moriah got brave and slowly struggled to her feet. Her thighs trembled immediately, and a wave pushed her, but she didn't tip. She worked hard every day and was in great shape, but paddle boarding required muscles she'd never known she had. She dug the paddle in the right side twice then gingerly lifted it over and pushed it through on the left side. It was slow progress, but she was doing it.

Turk and Adonis glided past.

"Good job, Mama." Turk called.

"You're looking great," Adonis said.

Moriah couldn't resist dancing. Shimmying her hips and abdomen, she said, "Yeah baby—Whoa!" She flipped into the water, catching a mouthful. She couldn't touch the bottom, but her lifejacket kept her head from going completely under. Salt water coated her tongue, and she spit it out and laughed at herself.

Adonis and Turk sidled up to her as she shoved her paddle on the board and held on to the side. She'd have to swim back to shallow water to get on again.

"You shouldn't a been dancin', Mama."

"You can dance anytime," Adonis said with a twinkle in his blue eyes.

"You ain't seen dancing yet, boy." She shot back at him.

He threw back his head and laughed. "I'm looking forward to it."

Moriah started kicking away from them. They followed, and within seconds, she could touch the sandy bottom. She pushed herself up onto her board. "Think I'll stay on my knees this time."

"Is this your first time?" Adonis asked.

"I'm a quick learner." She jutted out her chin, standing on shaky legs, even though she'd just said she'd stay on her knees.

"Good. Prove it by showing me some more dance moves."

Moriah stuck her tongue out at him, but she did give him one more shake of her hips.

He grinned. "Thank you, kindly, ma'am."

"Spoken like a true Southern gentleman."

"Through and through."

They paddled around for a while longer. Turk stood, pressing against Adonis' legs for stability. He really thought he was surfing when a wave would gently push them toward the shore. Luckily, the waves were mellow at this beach.

"Let's go get some food, Mama." Turk called out as he and Adonis circled her next to the far buoys.

"Sure, sweets."

"Can I come too?" Adonis asked.

They turned their boards in sync and paddled slowly as the waves helped them ride into shore.

"We don't usually eat with unknown men."

"Hey now. We're like old pals. Your son's ridden with me. You've danced for me."

Moriah couldn't help but laugh again.

Adonis grinned. "There it is. That's what I've been waiting for."

Moriah shook her head. The boards bumped against the shore and Turk jumped off, running toward their beach stuff. Moriah started to pull her board up on the beach. Adonis stopped her with a warm hand on her arm. "Please, let me."

She shaded her eyes with her hand and glanced up at him. "You're taking this gentleman thing to the extreme."

"You not only danced for me, you laughed for me ... twice."

Moriah had been dunked in the ocean and was sure any makeup had washed away and her hair was an extreme case of frizz right now, but she'd never felt so beautiful in her entire life.

He bent down a little closer. "You'll really show me all your dance moves?"

Moriah planted a hand on his chest to keep some distance, but it totally backfired. She wasn't sure when he'd unbuckled his life jacket but her hand landed on smooth skin and firm muscles. He was delectable. She dropped her hand fast and drummed up some attitude. "I never promised to show you my dance moves. I just told you I've got moves you've never seen."

His face stayed much too serious as those blue eyes darkened with a smolder. *Oh, heaven help me now.*

"I shouldn't have said that." She murmured. Her mama would die if she saw Moriah carrying on like this. Then she'd remind her that handsome, single men didn't date struggling mamas. "I'm a good Christian girl. I only dance for fun and to praise the Lord. Not to draw some unknown man in."

Adonis swallowed. She watched his Adam's apple bob as he glanced over her face. "Am I just 'some unknown man'?"

"Right now you are." She was taking leave of her good senses.

A rich, blond hottie. Hadn't she learned her lesson the last time she'd fallen for one? *Please, Lord, a little help and sanity would go a long way right now.*

"What if I got to know you a little better? Then would you dance for me?" He placed his hand on her arm, and warm currents shot through her.

"You could only be so lucky."

He laughed but thankfully removed his hand. "I knew you were a good Christian girl from the moment I saw you."

"Well, that's good. The good Lord done give me everything, so I hope I show my love for Him in my face."

"You do. It's in the way you smile and the way you treat everyone—from your little boy, to the waiter who brought you a drink, to the dark-haired idiot who hit on you earlier today. Thanks for sending him packing by the way."

"How long have you been watching me?" *Honestly.* That was flattering, but a little bit overwhelming.

"Just the length of a dozen volleyball games."

Moriah's eyes widened. She had to look away from his penetrating gaze. Conveniently, she had the perfect excuse of checking on her boy. Turk was happy as could be, zooming his truck around. He seemed to have forgotten about being hungry.

"You said you don't dance to draw men in?"

"That's right," she whispered, glancing back up at him. She'd made that mistake and then thought she was in love. Now, she was much more wary and in touch with her Savior. Her dancing wasn't about being sensual, but extracting happiness from each moment of life. She used it to celebrate and praise the Lord.

"You don't have to try to draw me in." Adonis moistened his lips and then whispered, "I'm already there."

Moriah swallowed hard. She didn't spend much time with men outside of her circle at church and those who stayed at the

Cloverdale. To have this devastatingly handsome man not only looking at her like she was heaven, but admitting that he was already drawn in? This was not good. Normally, her chest would tighten, and she'd be ready to run, but right now, she just wanted him to keep looking at her and whispering sweet nonsense. She needed to escape now before she lost her good sense completely. He was probably just looking for a vacation hookup, and that was not her at all. "Turk? Shall we go eat?"

"Shore!" He jumped up, clutching his truck. "Can we come back to our track after?"

"Shore." She smiled at him and ruffled his curls.

"We could order right here." Adonis suggested.

"I can keep playing?" Turk asked. "Thank you, surfer guy!" He raced back to his track. "I want chicken nuggets, fries, ketchup, and a Coke. Thank you, Mama!"

Adonis signaled a waiter and placed Turk's order, asking him, "Which kind of coke, Turk?"

"Sprite, please!"

Even if his accent had been scrubbed from him, Moriah now knew he truly was from the South, where every soft drink was a "coke." Adonis turned to her. Moriah wasn't sure if she should get ticked at him again or maybe touch his chest one more time before she told him to buzz off. The waiter and Adonis were both staring at her, and Moriah couldn't take it much longer. "I'll have a hamburger, fries, and one of those delicious Miami Vice drinks. Thank you kindly." She wasn't used to being waited on.

The waiter winked and turned to Adonis.

"Oh, can you make it without alcohol?" Moriah asked quickly.

Adonis cocked an eyebrow at her. "You *are* a good Christian girl."

"You know it." She lifted her hands, twirled a circle, and wiggled her hips and abdomen like a belly dancer. She hoped it wasn't too provocative to do that move wearing tight boy shorts and a halter top.

The waiter laughed, and Adonis stared with open admiration.

"No poison?" the waiter asked. "But you look like so much fun."

"This is one hundred percent natural fun," Moriah said, dancing a little bit more. She always danced. Why did Adonis watching her make it so much more intimate?

Adonis placed his order. Then he rested his hand on her lower back and escorted her toward the lounge chairs by Turk's track. His palm touching her bare skin was heavenly. She'd thought they were coming to paradise on this trip, but she'd had no clue that heaven included a man like this. How in the world was she going to stay strong? After the boy she'd loved her entire life ditched her when she was pregnant and barely seventeen, she'd stayed far away from men, not ready to risk her or Turk's hearts. Especially with a handsome blond guy with blue eyes and a huge wallet. Okay, she was making an assumption about the oversized pocketbook. Her Adonis just seemed like the type, and he wouldn't be staying here without one. He seemed too confident to be on someone else's dime like she was.

"I should probably ask your name since I don't eat with unknown women," Adonis said.

Moriah laughed. She couldn't help it. "I don't need to know your name—you're Adonis."

"What? Adonis?" He chuckled. "What does that mean?"

"The Greek god of beauty and desire."

He laughed louder now. "Well, thank you. I feel flattered."

"You should."

"So you don't even want to know my real name?" He leaned closer to her, and her breath caught.

"Nah. Stay all mysterious and hot for me, will you?"

"Whatever I can do to stay by your side."

Why did he have some obsession with her? A man like this could have any woman anywhere. Why her? Seriously, he was probably just a schmoozer who wanted a vacation fling. She glanced around for his friends, but the volleyball court was deserted.

"Okay." She needed to cut the flirting. "Actually, tell me your name, and I'll tell you mine."

"You first."

"Moriah Jackson. Pleased to meet you." She stood and bowed for him.

Adonis grasped her hand and said, "I'd like another dance much better than the bow."

"Stop." Moriah pushed a hand at him and sat down again.

"I've never seen anyone move like you."

"You don't get out much?"

"Not really."

She highly doubted that. "Well, my friend, you haven't seen nothin' yet and I'm not trying to brag or be suggestive. I just know how to move."

He grinned. "I can see that. So what time are we going dancing tonight?"

"I don't even know your name." She smiled at him, but he was pushing her a little bit harder than she was comfortable with.

"Jace Browning. Pleased to meet you, ma'am. Commitment to dancing now?"

"Turk isn't real fond of clubs." She smiled, pleased that she'd dodged that bullet though she would've loved to go dancing, especially with him.

"We can have our own private dance." He leaned toward her. "I can get rid of my brothers, and Turk can watch a show in one of the rooms in the suite while you teach me how to move my hips like you do."

"Oh, my goodness, you are incorrigible."

He leaned back against the cushioned beach lounge and grinned. "Does that mean yes?"

"No. I'm here with some friends. We have plans tonight." She honestly wasn't sure what he was suggesting, but there was no way she was going to his suite when she hardly knew him.

"Doing what?"

"Dinner. It takes hours apparently." These chairs were really comfy, and the shade made it the perfect temperature. She was having a great time flirting with him while Turk played happily in the sand next to them.

"Tomorrow?" His blue eyes were full of pleading.

"We're going to Explore Park."

"What a coincidence. So am I."

"You are not." She glared at him and folded her arms across her chest.

"I am now."

"Okay, there's a line between hot and stalkerish, and you're flirting with it."

His smile disappeared. "Oh. I'm sorry. I've just never met anyone like you."

"You've never met a single mama who knows how to dance? I thought you said you were from Bama?"

"Grew up there. Went to college in upstate New York and then started my business. It's based in Alabama, but I travel a lot."

"Interesting. What's your business?" She glanced at Turk. He was still happy with his truck and the sand.

"Financial planning. Nothing too exciting."

"Are you here for business?"

"Not my business. Corporate retreat for my parents' company."

"Oh? So the whole family's here?" She focused on the waves softly rolling onto the beach, not liking the thought of meeting his family. Would his mother immediately snub Moriah and Turk?

"Only my brothers. My mom has adult onset diabetes. They don't travel much anymore."

"I saw some other men who look like you." She felt bad for pre-judging his mom when the woman wasn't healthy. Maybe she wasn't snobbish and hurtful like Brock's mom had been.

His mouth drew in a thin line. "Those would be my brothers."

"You don't seem too thrilled to be with them."

"They're good guys." He shrugged. "What about you? Is your family in Montgomery?"

"Yes. My brother Harrison is just finishing up his last year at Auburn. He's a wide receiver, and he's getting his master's in accounting, all on scholarship."

"Wow. You sound very proud."

"I'm the proudest sister this side of the Mississippi." She blushed as she realized how far the river was from here.

"And your parents?"

"My mama is a good old Southern mama. She cooks up a storm trying to feed the countryside, and she has dance moves that put mine to shame."

"Of course she does." He smiled gently at her. "What about your father?"

"My daddy's as skinny as my mama is wide, and he works hard to take care of everybody. He's an electrician." Might as well make sure he knew the discrepancy in their social status before this went much farther. She was more certain than ever that he was a richie.

"Are you here with your family?"

"No. My good friends who are also my bosses."

The waiter came and interrupted their conversation. Moriah

was busy after that helping Turk eat and balancing all the food and drinks on the small table at the end of her lounge chair. She glanced at Jace. It was a good name, but Adonis still fit him better. She'd teased him about becoming stalkerish. Hopefully, that would dissuade him from trying to spend too much time around her. She wouldn't mind spending more time with him, but even if he was from Alabama and she might be able to see him after the vacation, she didn't need the distraction right now. Things were going great managing the bed and breakfast and raising her cute boy. No, a good-looking white man who would more than likely break her heart was definitely not in the plans.

Find *Cancun Getaway* on Amazon.

EXCERPT FROM THE IRRESISTIBLE GROOM

Claire Tucker's three-inch heels tapped a quick pattern as she rushed across the laminate flooring toward the exterior doors of the yoga studio.

"See you tomorrow," Hallie, the young front desk attendant called.

"Yes, you will." Claire grinned, waved, and pushed at the front doors. She was at the five a.m. power yoga class every weekday morning at Holistic Studios. The state-of-the-art yoga studio also had locker rooms and clean showers so she could be ready and to work in her downtown Dallas office by six-thirty. Work was her life and that was fine by her.

With the fast pace of her life and business, she needed this break to ground herself. Especially when she had days like yesterday where she'd had to call security to remove a hulking football player, who couldn't take no for an answer, from her office. She didn't date much and she especially didn't date jerks who thought every woman wanted them. A shudder ran through her as she remembered his thick arms surrounding her like steel bands. Luckily her sharp fingernails and the panic button under her desk had done the trick. She doubted he'd get those scratches on his face healed anytime soon.

A man caught the door and held it open for her.

"Thank you," Claire murmured, glancing at him. Her breath caught and she paused in the open doorway. "Brig?" Brig Hunsaker was her client, Knox Sherman's head of security and she had the hugest crush on him. She always kept it under control because there was no way she'd again fall for a man whose job description entailed putting himself in constant danger. Peyton's face swam through her mind but she pushed it back out again. It had been three years and she'd healed and forgiven herself —sort of.

"Claire." A huge smile made Brig's cheeks crinkle.

He had a smooth, perfectly handsome face, blue eyes, prematurely gray hair, and an incredibly built body. He was so smoking hot Claire had trouble thinking straight around him. She berated herself for it constantly. She was a sports agent and her clients were all buff and most of them were extremely good-looking. None of them had turned her head, except for Brady Giles, who was now happily married, but she knew now that her former crush on Brady was a mere Dum-dum sucker compared to a pound of Ghirardelli milk chocolate with sea salt and caramel when she looked at Brig. How was she going to stay strong around him? He'd tried to ask her out quite a few times when she'd been at Knox and Ema's house and she'd always been able to change the subject quickly or tease and get away.

"Hey, Brig. What are you doing here?"

"I teach a Tae Kwon Do class at seven-thirty. Came early today to work out some kinks before class."

Claire couldn't resist glancing over the muscles revealed in his gray tank top. Sheesh. Why did she have to be so drawn to the buff types? Most of the time that meant athletes—off limits because of her career as a sports agent; muscle heads—off limits because the steroids had fried their brains; or men who protected and served—off limits because she wasn't going there ever again.

But, my, oh, my, Brig looked good. No harm in looking, so long as she didn't think about throwing all her chips in the pot.

"Good to see you." She walked out the door. He didn't give her much room and her shoulder brushed his muscular chest. He smelled like musk and soap—definitely all man. A smoldering warmth started in the pit of her stomach. *Move faster, sister.* It was still dark outside this early in the morning, but the city lights illuminated the sidewalk.

"Wait." Brig released the door and jogged to her side.

Claire took some calming breaths, trying to center herself. She needed another yoga class.

Brig touched her arm and no amount of breathing could prevent her from noticing how good his touch felt. It was like rocky road ice cream in a waffle cone on a hot Texas day.

Claire turned to him. He stared at her with those bright blue eyes and she wanted to trip on her Kate Spade stilettos and see if he caught her. She hated being short so she always wore the tallest heels she could get away with. She was a powerful, career-driven woman and the lift bolstered her confidence. Brig wasn't as tall as Knox or Brady or some of her other burly clients, who most likely had some form of gigantism. He was about five-eleven, the perfect height in her book. Instead of feeling small and looked-down-upon, she felt protected by his tough manliness. *Stop it, Claire. You're not going there.*

She waited for him to say something. He was the one who'd chased her down and called for her to wait, right?

A muscle worked in his jaw as he looked down at his hand on

her arm and then back into her eyes. "Everything about you is so perfect," he said softly.

Claire arched an eyebrow, trying to look at ease while her heart was slamming against her chest. How could she resist him? He was flawless in her eyes and he'd just said she was perfect. He reeled her in like she was a guppy on a hook large enough a thousand pound marlin couldn't escape from it.

He released her arm and jammed a hand through his hair. It melted her heart that this military man could be affected by her as he mussed his own hair and studied the pavement. She loved his gray hair. It set him apart. She loved his calm persona and confidence more than his looks, and that was really saying something because his looks were perfect to her.

"Things don't come out right when I'm around you," he muttered.

Claire was ecstatic that he'd just admitted that. "So the tough, fine-looking body guard has a weakness?" Dang she shouldn't have said that, it was like she was egging him on.

Brig's slow smile did funny things to her stomach. "Yeah. You're definitely my weakness."

She returned his smile. It thrilled her that she threw him off his game. He was a stud from his head to his toes—confidence and ability radiated from him and he'd just said she was his weakness. *Oh, help.*

She had to step back or she might do something really stupid, like ask him out. "Everybody has to have one. You know? Superman and Kryptonite." She spun on her heels and headed toward the crosswalk. "See ya." Flinging her hand up, she ground her teeth in frustration when she noticed the traffic light had turned green and the crosswalk was a solid red hand.

Glancing over her shoulder, she saw Brig striding deliberately to her side. *Dang it, dang it, dang it. Say no, be strong. Oh, good night, I love a confident man. He's too stinking appealing for my own good.*

Claire ignored him as he came so close his arm brushed hers and that musky man smell swirled in her nostrils. Yum. Forget breakfast, she only wanted Brig. No! She needed to move. The downtown Dallas street was quiet this early in the morning. Maybe she should run across on a green light and pray she didn't get tagged by some errant vehicle.

"Kryptonite hurt Superman. I don't think you'd hurt me," he said in a low rumble.

Claire couldn't resist turning to look at him. "You have no idea how wrong you are. There would be nothing but hurt in store for you and I." Her stomach curdled. Hurt? What would he say if he knew she was responsible for her fiancé's death? She knew more about hurt than anyone and she wouldn't allow herself to destroy Brig like she'd destroyed Peyton.

Brig's smooth brow wrinkled and his blue eyes looked troubled. "You're wrong, Claire, please give me a chance. Just one date."

Claire took a steadying breath and shook her head. She couldn't hold his gaze. Why did he have to look like she'd hurt him already? If only he knew. It was so much smarter to keep her distance. Head of security, military man. *No, thank you, may I please choose again?*

The traffic light turned to yellow and she took the out, rushing across the crosswalk. Staring at the pavement, she prayed she could get away and he wouldn't come after her. Tears pricked at the corners of her eyelids and that made her angry. How dare Brig worm his way into her heart with his kindness and patience? She was protecting him as much as herself. He had no clue how twisted her heart was and what she'd done to the last man she'd claimed to love.

A screech of brakes startled her out of her misery. Her head whipped up to see headlights bearing down on her. She screamed and tried to hurry out of their path but her tight skirt and heels were working against her. *Please help*, she screamed a prayer as she heard Brig calling out her name.

Available July 17, 2018

ALSO BY CAMI CHECKETTS

Navy Seal Romance

The Protective Warrior

The Captivating Warrior

Billionaire Beach Romance

Shadows in the Curtain

Caribbean Rescue

Cozumel Escape

Cancun Getaway

Onboard for Love

Trusting the Billionaire

How to Kiss a Billionaire

Billionaire Bride Pact Romance

The Resilient One

The Feisty One

The Independent One

The Protective One

The Faithful One

The Daring One

Park City Firefighter Romance

Rescued by Love

Reluctant Rescue

Stone Cold Sparks

Other Books by Cami

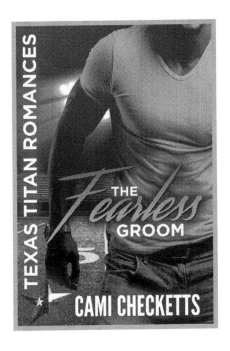

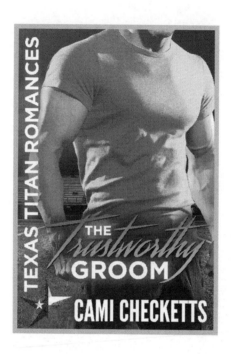

The Beastly Groom: Texas Titan Romance

Made in the USA
Columbia, SC
05 August 2023

21295708R00083